DEATH ON NANTUCKET

DEATH ON NANTUCKET

FRANCINE

MATHEWS

SOHO CRIME

Published by
Soho Press, Inc.
853 Broadway
New York, NY 10003

Library of Congress Cataloging-in-Publication Data

Mathews, Francine.
Death on Nantucket / Francine Mathews.
A Merry Folger Nantucket mystery ; 5

ISBN 978-1-61695-737-7
eISBN 978-1-61695-738-4

1. Folger, Merry (Fictitious character)—Fiction. 2. Nantucket
Island (Mass.)—Fiction. 3. Murder—Investigation—Fiction.
4. Women detectives—Fiction. I. Title.
PS3563.A8357 D44 2017 813'.54—dc23
2016047184

Printed in the United States of America

10 9 8 7 6 5 4 3 2 1

To Mark,
for all the memories of small boys and sand

DEATH ON NANTUCKET

Prologue

THE SHADOW OF the Cessna flitted over the white-capped waves of Nantucket Sound, swift and elusive as a gull's wing. Nora could see the shape of the island long before it spread beneath them, dark green and brown in the surrounding blue. She was sitting near the front of the Cape Air plane, which was the size of a minivan. Its passengers were usually distributed among its nine seats by weight, but on this sunny May morning there were only three people flying to Nantucket. The pilot told them they could sit where they liked. Nora chose the starboard wing. She was hoping to glimpse the house's gray-shingled eaves as they flew over the harbor.

There was the jetty, trailing out into the Sound like a pinball flipper. There, far below, was the car ferry from Hyannis steaming into its wharf. No sails braved the stiff wind that raked the sea today, and the moorings in the basin were deserted. Summer People and their yachts had yet to arrive. But the steeples of the old churches on Centre and Orange Streets still pierced the horizon in a way she remembered.

When she craned to study the roofs above Steps Beach, however, Nora was suddenly disoriented. There were so many houses, now, where once there had been only a few. Raw scars in the bluff and naked wood frames showed that more were rising. Huge houses with swimming pools—swimming pools, on Nantucket!—stretched out behind them. Compounds with guest cottages and caretaker quarters above expansive garages. What did people do with so much space? Although Step Above, the house where she'd spent each summer as a child, was hardly small . . .

The plane dipped and bucked as the pilot descended. The harbor fell away behind. Nora gripped the seat, her stomach lurching into her throat as the ground came up to meet them. No matter how many bush planes or choppers she caught, in hellholes or paradises around the world, this was what she remembered each time she landed: a runway bracketed by beach plum and sand.

"YOU IN FOR the Wine Festival?" her taxi driver asked.

"The what?"

"Wine Festival. Whole world's coming in this weekend. It's the summer kickoff."

"Not Memorial Day?"

"Too obvious." His eyes met hers in the rearview mirror. An embroidered flourish on his polo shirt read *Kevin*. This was Kevin's Island Taxi, so apparently she'd scored the owner himself. A tribute to Tuesday mornings, off-season.

"The Chamber of Commerce likes to make up reasons to celebrate," he explained.

"Like Daffodil Weekend. Or Christmas Stroll," Nora said.

"And the Book Festival, the Dance Festival, the Film

Festival." Kevin shrugged. "Now it's wine. I'm waiting for them to organize Oktoberfest, myself, but knowing the Chamber it'll probably be Craft Brews, and I can't get behind that. Why pay six bucks a bottle when you like your beer on tap?"

The taxi bucketed over Main Street's cobblestones. Nora glanced swiftly right and left, taking it all in. Scaffolding surrounded the aged brick of the Pacific Club at the foot of the street, and Ralph Lauren had taken over the space that used to belong to Nantucket Looms, but the compass rose painted on the side of the building still showed the nautical miles to Pitcairn Island—14,300. Crazy Quinn's ice cream store was gone, she realized, as they lurched across the cobblestones to Water Street. How long had she been away?

"Lincoln Circle," Kevin mused as he turned up Cobblestone Hill. "Spence Murphy lives around there. The foreign correspondent. Probably before your time, and he's getting pretty old, now—but that guy will always be a personal hero to me. Staying behind after we pulled out of Laos. He blew the whole secret war wide open, you know? The FBI had a file on him, he was considered so dangerous."

"They had files on a lot of people, back then," Nora replied.

"What's the address you're looking for?"

"Thirty-two Lincoln. Place called Step Above."

Kevin glanced at her again in the rearview mirror. "But that's Murphy's place, isn't it? You *know* him?"

Nora felt her usual weariness. Here on Nantucket she shouldn't have to explain. "He's my dad, actually."

"Your dad?" Kevin's eyes widened. He was trying to

make sense of it: her delicate frame, jet-black hair, her almond-shaped eyes. She had never looked like a Murphy and never would.

"I'm adopted."

He almost missed the granite stone marker at the foot of the crushed quahog shell drive. She'd heard the house had been winterized when her parents moved permanently on-island, but the hedges hadn't been trimmed in years. The sprawling old captain's house needed re-shingling and the *rosa rugosa* had run amok next to the garage.

Some things, she thought with a rush of gratitude as she handed Kevin his fare and stepped out of the taxi, never changed at all. Some things you could count on. Some things were safe.

That was why, despite all the heartache and hatred, she had finally decided to come home.

Kevin waved and pulled out of the circular drive. Nora shouldered her backpack. It held all she owned in the world. She lifted her head and took the tricky first step toward the front door.

Chapter One

"IT'S ABSOLUTELY PERFECT," Meredith Folger
said as she gazed at herself in the full-length mirror. She
was standing in the sunlit master bedroom of an old house
built in 1821 by a man named Thomas Mason, who had
captained the *Leah* out of Nantucket until his death in
the South Pacific in 1843. The house on Cliff Road, faced
with narrow white clapboards and topped with a square
walk on its roof, was lapped in green lawns and hedges
and buffered by opulent hydrangeas. It had come down
through the centuries in the Mason family, who used it
only during the summer months now. From the windows
that drenched the room in sunshine, Merry could look
out over the back terrace and its pergola to the wet-paint
smear of the harbor, which was flooded with boat traffic
on this first day of July. The expanse of Jetties Beach was
clearly visible. Happy people were stretched out on its
sand and kites rippled over its dunes. But Merry wasn't
admiring the million-dollar view. She had eyes only for
herself, and the extraordinary gown Mayling Stern had
just slipped carefully over her blonde head.

It was pale silk chiffon of a shade somewhere between
cream and chartreuse that brought out the vivid green of
her eyes. Mayling had cut a curvaceous column with a

classically elegant bodice that framed Merry's collarbone like a Renaissance portrait. The back plunged in a low V. The hem stopped just above the ankle strap of her shoe. It was a grown-up wedding dress for a woman past thirty who had no interest in presenting herself as the heroine of a Disney fairy tale. Over the past few months, Meredith had seen every bridal salon in Boston, high-priced and low, and despaired of finding anything that was not billowing or farcical. The fashion appeared to favor voluminous skirts and jeweled bodices. She refused to speak her vows to Peter Mason across three feet of pendulous hoop, like Scarlett O'Hara, as she'd told Mayling bitterly one night over dinner at Dune.

"Here's what you want," the designer said coolly, as she sketched red lipstick swiftly over her white napkin. "Severe. Yet timeless. Like the walls of this room."

It was a composition of maybe five lines. A dress not for a bride, Merry thought, but a dress to get *married* in. She met Mayling's eyes. "Are you serious?"

"Of course. I've always wanted to do bridal."

"What would it . . ." She swallowed, not sure how to ask the price of a New York designer's bridal fling. Fifteen thousand dollars? Twenty? "I mean, would this be couture level?"

"In terms of cost?" Mayling's eyes slid over to Peter, whose hand cupped Meredith's shoulder. "I thought you were marrying money. But never mind. For a friend—a friend I'm experimenting on . . . *such* a deal, as my father, Maury, used to say. I'll throw in the fabric at cost, as a wedding gift."

Merry took the napkin home. She taped it to a whiteboard above her police station desk, where it hovered in her peripheral vision as she scrolled through databases. In April, she had her first fitting in Mayling's muslin model—something she hadn't expected and was unable to assess.

But here, in the graceful light of the old and beloved house, she saw the actual gown for the first time.

On herself.

And she was exquisite.

Elegant. Confident.

Unrecognizable?

"Hold still," Mayling said through a mouthful of pins. She pinched a miniscule amount of silk at an almost-invisible seam. Merry tried not to breathe.

A woman's laughter drifted up from the center hallway—Georgiana Whitney, Peter's sister, who was staying in the house for the next month. Then Peter's voice, the words indistinguishable.

"Don't let him in," Merry said tensely.

Mayling lifted her head. "That bad?"

The designer had brought the dress to Cliff Road because Merry was stealing time for the fitting from one of her busiest weeks. It was Friday, July 1st, the day before Nantucket would launch its annual Fourth of July weekend celebrations. That meant road races tomorrow—Peter was competing in one—fireworks off Jetties Beach the night of July 3rd, and Main Street morning activities (complete with water fights between rival firemen crews, pie-eating contests, and crying babies) on the Fourth.

The acknowledged nightmare of the entire weekend, however, was a spontaneous event the Town Council hadn't sanctioned or funded, or could possibly control—the Nobadeer Beach Party. This was a recent phenomenon that had grown over the years through social media. Thousands upon thousands of high school and college kids poured off the ferries with cases of beer or drove over the sand in permitted vehicles and took over Nobadeer Beach on Nantucket's South Shore. They arrived early in the day and stayed until the police shut them down. This was usually around dinnertime, at which point many of the kids were passed out from alcohol poisoning or drug overdoses or too many selfies in the sun. Ambulances carried the casualties to Nantucket Cottage Hospital, which was invariably overwhelmed. Partiers peed on local residents' lawns, trashed their patio umbrellas and cars, left enormous piles of garbage on the beach, and—memorably—invaded empty houses to have sex on strangers' couches. Merry and her fellow police officers were expected to contain and control the hordes, but when they tried to discourage more cars or people from walking onto Nobadeer, the spontaneous bash simply moved to a different beach elsewhere on the island. It was a significant headache because it strained the Nantucket police during a weekend when they were already challenged by the crowds on Main Street. They were forced to bring in extra Community Service Officers and police by the dozens from the mainland.

But that all began tomorrow. Today, Merry had agreed to meet George and Peter at the Cliff Road house before all Independence Day hell broke loose. Mayling arrived half an hour early. Merry thought that would give her enough time to fit the dress. But now she didn't want to take it off. And she didn't want Peter to see it before The Day.

She groped for Mayling's hands, her smile incandescent, her eyes blurring with tears. "Lock the door."

"You're welcome," Mayling said.

THE UNCONVENTIONAL GOWN changed everything about a wedding Meredith had secretly been dreading.

It gave her courage to defy Peter's formidable mother, who lived permanently on Park Avenue, and veto a New York ceremony. It allowed her to blithely decline a reception at the Pierre. Merry and Peter would be married in the soaring clarity of the old Congregational church on Centre Street, and walk up to the Cliff Road house afterward, followed by their friends. Tess Starbuck would cater the food, which would be fresh and locally sourced and utterly delectable. Mayling's husband, Sky Jackson, had ordered cases of wine and champagne from the vineyard owners who'd impressed him most during the Wine Festival in May.

"You should carry arum lilies," Mayling said now, eyeing her critically. "The cream ones, with chartreuse throats. Perfect with this silk. The little girls can have late hydrangeas."

"—In Ralph's lightship baskets," Merry supplied. Ralph Waldo Folger was her grandfather. The little girls were Georgiana's daughters. They would get to miss a day of school, at least, to fly in from Connecticut for the September wedding. Their two brothers were equally happy to cut class for Uncle Peter.

"Meredith!" Peter called.

"Coming!"

She helped Mayling tuck her wedding gown back into its protective silk bag, her fingers lingering on the zipper.

"We'll do one last session a week out from the date," Mayling warned, "in case you've somehow lost or gained weight dramatically in the interim. But tell me right now if there's anything about the dress you can't live with."

"Just the months until September," Merry said.

Mayling smiled fleetingly. She was not the most expressive of women, but Merry had learned that she cared deeply about the few people she allowed into her life. "Those weeks will fly, girlfriend. And you've got so much to do between now and then. Not to mention work."

"Work." Merry glanced at her phone. "Damn. I've got a meeting at the station in half an hour. And Peter downstairs."

"Go," Mayling said, and unlocked the bedroom door.

GEORGIANA AND HER brother were sprawled on the twin white sofas that flanked the old fireplace. The chairs surrounding them were covered in varying shades of green and blue linen, some faded by sun, and the aqueous light filtering through the windows gave the entire space a floating quality. Down-filled pillows with old needlepoint covers were scattered among the seat cushions and tossed on the floor, probably by George's kids or their exuberant Labrador. Nothing was too precious to touch or scuff or treat carelessly in this place, despite the excellent provenance of the tables dotting the room or the nineteenth-century oils on its walls. For nearly two centuries it had been a family house, worn and loved. Merry was comfortable here as she never quite was in the Mason homes on the mainland.

"We were talking about the tent," George said as Merry crossed the hall and sank down beside Peter.

His hand came around her shoulders. "George wants one."

"Because of rain."

"Of course," George said patiently. "September's usually fine, but who knows? We could get a hurricane."

"In which case, we'll gather in here around the fireplace," Merry suggested.

"It'll be pretty crowded."

"Fifty people?" This was the intimate number of guests Merry and Peter had negotiated. None of his extended family's friends. Just people they both knew and loved. "This room could hold twice that. They'll spill into the hall."

"And the dining room," Peter pointed out.

"Where do you put the dance floor?" George asked reasonably. "And the band?"

"The *what?*" Peter's look of dismay was priceless. "Can't we just have a jazz trio for background noise over the champagne and hors d'oeuvres?"

"You're not going to dance with your bride?"

He glanced at Merry. "Does the bride want me to?"

"The bride thinks it's a shame," Merry replied, "to crowd the back lawn and block this spectacular harbor view with an enormous white elephant that costs around ten thousand dollars to erect and dismantle."

His dark brows flew up. "Are you serious?"

"I am."

"Good God. Merry's right, George—we'll huddle around the fire if it rains."

"Suit yourself." George kept her eyes on a notepad list she was compiling. "Just remember you have about a week to change your mind. After that, late fees apply."

"Three months ahead of time?" Merry said, aghast.

"This is a destination wedding location. Heavily booked. That ten-thousand-dollar dance will cost closer to fifteen if you wait too long."

"I'll take you to a nightclub on our honeymoon," Peter whispered.

"Deal," Merry said.

"One more thing." George was looking carefully at Merry now. "Check with your dad. Not about the cost—that's between you and Peter. But about *John's* dance. His waltz with his only daughter—his only *child*—under a spotlight on her wedding night. Ask your grandfather whether he's planning to whirl you around the floor, too. Because Ralph has the look of a proper gent. I wouldn't put it past him to tango with my mother."

"Oh, geez," Merry sighed, and put her face in her hands. Because of course George was right. Merry's own mother was dead. Both John Folger and Ralph Waldo would think it necessary to send her off properly, and hold up the Folger end in the face of Mason millions.

"There's no way round it, is there?" Peter asked.

"None," George said complacently. "Now, about the valet parking . . ."

Chapter Two

JOHN FOLGER, THE former chief of Nantucket Police, parked his Jeep Wrangler near the Boat Basin and ambled contentedly through the tangle of tourists disembarking from the fast ferry. July Fourth weekend might be the most crowded and demanding of the summer, but he was blessedly unconcerned this year. He cared nothing for the Nobadeer Beach Party or its headaches. He wove past the Vineyard Vines store and made his way down Water Street, a man completely at ease.

He was headed for a small shingle-covered cottage set on the pilings of Old North Wharf, one of the most picturesque and unspoiled spots to be found on the harbor. The Wharf Rat Club had a bright blue door framed in roses and hydrangeas. Its select group of members was male and female, islanders and Summer People, as it had been for over a hundred years; but a motto over the door proclaimed the club's simple philosophy: *No Seats Reserved for the Mighty.* Influence could not get you into the Wharf Rats. Good fellowship and affability did.

Portraits of past commodores and paintings of ships were ranged over the rough walls, with nautical charts and quarterboards from long-vanished vessels mounting to the rafters. The cottage had once been a quahog depot and Coffin's Marine supply store for local fishermen, who held down the chairs around its potbellied stove, trading stories over their coffee mugs. President Franklin Roosevelt had sailed his yacht *Amberjack* into harbor during his first term and was immediately inducted as a member. So were writers and artists, sailors and ambassadors, Supreme Court Justice William J. Brennan, scientists, professors, scallopers, lightship-basket weavers, and a few sharks of American industry. Coffin's store had disappeared long ago; now the stove and the room belonged entirely to the Wharf Rats. Their triangular black burgee sported a jaunty white rat smoking a pipe; it snapped vigorously in the breeze. Members wore the insignia pinned on their lapels and flew it on their boats and lawns.

John's father, Ralph Waldo Folger, had been a member of the club for over thirty years. John himself had been inducted only a month before. Until his resignation from the police force in January, he hadn't had time to kick back with his friends on a summer afternoon.

The club's front door was propped open. So was the back door, which offered a fresh view of the harbor and Steamboat Wharf. A few faces floated in the murk between the two oblongs of light. One of them was Ralph's. He was seated in an old wooden captain's chair, engrossed in conversation. He turned as John threw himself into a chair beside him.

"I was telling Spence," he said without preamble, "that we ran into Nora a few weeks back. At the grocery store. You remember."

"Nora." John glanced over at Ralph's friend, his eyes

adjusting to the dimness of the club interior. It was Spence Murphy, the celebrated foreign correspondent, in pressed chinos and a flat cap over his sparse gray hair. He wore an ancient field vest lined with pockets, a remnant from his reporting days.

John remembered Nora, now—a slim half-Asian girl Ralph had hailed at the Stop & Shop deli counter. Spence's adopted daughter, he'd said.

"Right. Nora. How long is she staying with you?"

"Who?" Spence asked, glancing from John to Ralph.

"Nora," Ralph said more loudly, as though Spence were deaf. "Your daughter."

Murphy shook his head slowly. "I haven't seen her in years. And who's this young man?"

Ralph seemed taken aback. His white brows furled speculatively over his blue eyes.

"I'm John Folger, sir. Ralph Waldo's son."

"That's grand," Murphy said heartily. "Pleased to meet you. Are you going to join the Rats one day, too?"

John frowned slightly. He'd been acquainted with Spencer Murphy for years, as he was with all of Ralph's cronies, and Murphy had helped induct him into the club last month. "I'd be honored, of course," he said.

Ralph clapped Spence on the back. "For now we'll just give him coffee."

John followed his father across the room to the mugs and creamer and the fresh smell of ground roasted beans. For reasons he didn't like to examine, he was relieved to see that Ralph's white beard was neatly trimmed, his collar sharply turned, his hands steady on the cup. His father was in his high eighties but remained a force to be reckoned with.

"Sad," Ralph murmured gruffly as he poured a mug. "Spence's mind is slipping. I've suspected as much, but he's managed to cover it pretty well. Compensate. They do, you know—in the early stages."

"Have you talked to his daughter about it? He has sons somewhere, too, doesn't he?"

"Boston and New York. But Spence lives alone. Barbara—his wife—died last year. He has a day woman come in, do his laundry, leave him dinner, that sort of thing. I suppose Nora's not here anymore, since he says he hasn't seen her in a while. He loses track of time. And faces." Ralph followed Spence Murphy's slow progress toward the clubhouse door. "He was a brilliant news guy, you know. One of the Greats."

"I know."

"His book on the secret war in Laos is one I'll never forget."

In the Cage of the Pathet Lao," John said. "I've been meaning to read it, now that I've got more time on my hands. I'm sure it's better than the movie."

"His description of the pullout from Long Tieng—and his own capture by the Communist insurgency—are riveting. You know he was kept in a bamboo cage for months before he escaped? Incredible journalism."

"Particularly when you realize he had no military training. It's one thing to be a soldier in that situation, another to be a noncombatant. That's part of what makes his account so powerful," John mused. "It could have been any one of us. I've always wondered—if I'd made Billy talk to Spence before he enlisted for Iraq—"

"It wouldn't have changed anything," Ralph Waldo said gently. Billy was John's son, Ralph's grandson, Merry's older brother. He had died years ago in Fallujah. "Billy wanted to go."

"I know. But Spence knew so much about conflict. He had such moral authority." John poured milk into his coffee and took a tentative sip. "I doubt the US would have resettled so many Hmong refugees after the Secret War if he hadn't stirred the public's outrage. He's one of those reporters who kept us honest."

"Nora's half-Hmong, you know. He brought her back on a later trip to the country—he was doing a report on the aftermath of the Hmong genocide. Trying to find out what happened to his Lao interpreter."

"His memories must be harrowing."

"His memories." Ralph's expression was somber. He glanced over his shoulder at Spence, who was staring blankly into space. "I wonder if he recognizes his own titles anymore. If I start to lose it, son, promise me you'll shove me out to sea. Put me in a boat and keep the oars. I don't want to come back."

"Dad." John grasped his father's shoulder.

Ralph sighed. "He's younger than I am. By a good four years. God, how I hate watching my friends grow old."

"Then let's get out of here," John suggested, "and go fishing."

He'd bought a powerboat when he retired. It was the first toy he'd treated himself to in years.

His father's face lit up. "Tuckernuck?"

"Why not?"

"I'd love to get over there again. It's been a while."

Tuckernuck was the small barrier island, only nine hundred acres, that trailed off the western end of Nantucket. It was separated from its larger neighbor by several hundred yards of ocean and only reachable by boat. There were bluefish grounds off Tuck that were well worth visiting.

John finished his mug of coffee and set it down near Ralph's. Without another word, the two men made for the door.

"THAT BLUEFISH STINKS," Elliot Murphy said. He rolled down the Audi's window and breathed deeply. Here was what he'd been missing in the summer stench of New York: salt ocean, roses, wild lavender, pine, and the dusky earth scent of sunstruck moors. The unmistakable smell of Nantucket. They were driving up Cobblestone Hill from the car ferry in a blaze of July sunshine. Andre had made him stop at the fish market on the way to the house.

"You're smelling hickory smoke." Andre's right hand grasped the leather ceiling strap as the car rocked over the roadbed. His other grasped the collar of their Westie, MacTavish. "And you love my pâté. So does Spence. Throw in some gin and lime and we won't need dinner."

"I've got reservations."

"Of course you do." He glanced at Elliot. "Are we taking Spence?"

"He won't want to come. He can't track our voices over the noise of a restaurant." It wasn't just Spence's hearing that was failing, of course—he had difficulty tracking *any* conversation these days. But Elliot left that thought unspoken. He didn't have to state the obvious to Andre.

Elliot pulled off Lincoln into Step Above's quahog shell drive. The grass strip down the middle was parched and weedy. The house's white trim was peeling. A garden hose snaked through the unmown lawn. Elliot surveyed the house with the sharp eye of the real estate agent he was. It had fifteen rooms, and sat on nearly an acre of land behind mature hedges in one of the most sought-after areas of the island. But the house needed re-shingling and a new roof. The privet hedges were wildly overgrown. It was far too valuable a property to neglect. He'd have to talk to Dad this week and set up some workmen while he was here.

Roseline's aged sedan was pulled up before the door. He felt a breath of relief; he'd forgotten she was coming every day, now. That meant the sheets had been changed and fresh towels put out. She'd have Dad's dinner ready, so there'd be no fuss when they left for town.

The Westie, MacTavish, jumped down from Andre's lap and bolted for the door. Roseline opened it a second later and Tav rose on his hind legs, panting in greeting.

"Mr. Elliot! Your father never told me you were coming!"

"No?" He'd called Spence last week. He'd thought his dad was pleased.

"And Mr. Andre!" Roseline put up her cheek to be kissed; she was fond of Elliot's partner. They were both of Haitian descent, although Andre was third-generation American and she had emigrated less than fifteen years before. "How long you two staying? It won't take a moment to put fresh sheets on your beds."

She maintained the fiction that they slept in separate rooms, joined by a shared bath.

"We're here through the holiday," Andre said. "Headed back July fifth."

"You should stay all summer." Her tone was decisive. "What else is this great house for? And Mr. Spence rattling around inside. Lord knows there's enough room. I'll take that bluefish."

She relieved Andre of his shopping bag.

"Is Dad here?"

"He's down at that club on the docks."

As though it were a sailor's bar, Elliot thought, and his father drinking all afternoon. He kissed Roseline on her other cheek. "We'll bring in our bags. Is there any iced tea?"

"Never mind that. I'll get out the gin," she told him.

HE FOUND ANDRE already opening the French doors from the living room to the backyard, and followed him. MacTavish ambled between their legs, his white muzzle probing for scent, making for the edge of the lawn. There was nothing between the house and the cliff but a wonky pair of plastic Adirondack chairs from Stop & Shop, grass tufting around their legs. An ashtray sat forgotten between them—a ceramic clamshell Elliot had made as a kid during summer camp, forty years ago. He hunkered down over it, frowning, and stirred the butts with a finger. They were several days old and soggy with rain. His father hadn't smoked in decades. So who—?

He glanced around. The blown remains of his dead mother's peonies nodded in ungainly clumps beside withered heads of iris. The roses were in flower; so were the ancient and glorious hydrangeas that ringed the far end of the lawn. There was an arched trellis there, matted with climbers. Its waist-high gate faced the harbor.

It was this single point in the whole extraordinary property that gave Step Above its real cachet, its singular advantage, and its immense value.

It overlooked Steps Beach.

This was just a loosely defined stretch of sand between Jetties Beach to the east and Dionis to the west. The harbor waves here were gentle and there was no undertow to speak of. It was a beach for building sand castles and eating box lunches brought from Something Natural on Cliff Road. And although it was technically public, few tourists found their way to Steps Beach in the high season. There was no parking lot, no changing rooms, showers or toilet facilities, no snack bar with congealing puddles of ketchup and stained paper napkins. No seagulls tearing soggy French fries from trash bins. Just a trail through the hedges from Lincoln Ave. to a lengthy pitch of wooden stairs, and the scent of wild roses on the wind.

Step Above, like all the privileged properties overlooking Steps Beach, had its own private set of stairs plunging down the steep cliff.

Andre joined Elliot at the trellis gate. His dark head brushed the dangling petals and released a flood of scent that washed over them both. With it came intense memories of childhood. Elliot closed his eyes and grasped Andre's hand, restraining him for a moment.

His mother, clipping these roses, the wind off the ocean teasing her strawberry-blonde hair. His father tackling him around the middle and carrying him, pell-mell, down to the first landing, and then the second and the third—the dizzying descent to the gully covered with moor scrub, the headlong race across the boardwalk to the dunes with their sharp grasses and prickly scrawl of salt-spray roses, flowering in vivid shades of pink against the dark green leaves.

The deep blue of the Sound beyond.

A few smooth granite pebbles and slipper shells under his bare feet. The shock of the ocean, curling his toes.

Andre's fingers squeezed his. "Let's go down. It's always magic, the first time each summer."

He opened the gate. MacTavish let out a bark and plummeted from step to step. Elliot followed him. For the first time in a long while he felt that he was home.

A HALF-HOUR AND a brisk walk later, Andre was busy in Roseline's kitchen, making smoked bluefish pâté. Chopped shallots, sour cream, a little mayonnaise, some sherry. Elliot grasped their overnight bags and carried them upstairs. MacTavish ran ahead of him.

His childhood room was sea-blue, and held twin beds he and Andre usually pushed together to form a king. The adjoining bath was narrow, old and tiled. It connected to a room painted pale yellow, a color Elliot hated. When Dad died, he planned to renovate the whole house. The other bedrooms on this floor would be restructured so that each had a private bath, but these two made a perfect Jack-and-Jill suite for kids, with beds built into the alcoves under the dormer windows like cabins on a ship.

He didn't ask himself whose kids would sleep in them.

He halted in the bedroom doorway, his sandy brows coming swiftly down over his blue eyes.

Someone else had already moved in.

A black sweater lay neatly folded over the back of a chair. A pair of paperbacks sat on the bedside table, along with a pen and a pack of cigarettes. There was another ashtray, too—a glass one, this time, lifted years ago from the Opera House restaurant, which no longer existed.

Elliot crossed swiftly to the bathroom and glanced inside.

Toiletries.

A woman's, by the look of them.

For an instant, he wondered if Roseline had been staying over, nights. If his father had been sick—

Or falling again?

"Roseline," he called.

She appeared in the doorway, folded sheets from the linen closet in her arms. "I'm putting you in the green bedroom, Mr. Elliot," she said. "Your sister's stuff is still in here."

"My *sister's*?"

He stared at her, aghast.

Nora had been gone for years. How many? More than seven, at least, because she'd never met Andre. Ten years? Twelve? She hadn't even come home for Mom's funeral—

"Did you say my *sister's* here?"

"She was," Roseline said. "Showed up at Wine Festival time. But she only stayed a few days. One morning I came, and she was just gone. Your father couldn't tell me where or when she'd be back. No message. Just a bit of laundry and all her things left behind. Maybe she found a friend?"

"Sounds like Nora," Elliot said bitterly. "Did she take all Dad's cash with her, too?"

"No." There was a hint of reproach in Roseline's voice. "I guess she'll be back, Mr. Elliot. Why would she leave her computer here, otherwise?"

It was strange, Elliot thought. Not that Nora had left, but that she'd ever arrived. He turned once in the middle of the room, as though he could summon his sister from under the bed. Then he picked up his suitcases and followed Roseline down the hall.

IT WAS MACTAVISH, in the end, who found her.

Andre had finished his pâté and thought it high time the drinks were poured. He came looking for Elliot and caught Tav scratching and whiffling at a closed door in the upstairs hallway. He clutched the Westie firmly around the middle, but Tav struggled free and shoved his nose under the doorjamb. When Andre reached for him again, he barked sharply in protest.

"You won't believe this," Elliot was saying as he came into the hall, but Andre had already opened Tav's door and the dog shot up the flight of steps behind it.

"That's not safe," Roseline called. "The floorboards have rotted."

Andre swung up the steps, Elliot after him.

Tav had stopped short in the middle of the attic. His paws rested on the third rung of a folding stair let down from the ceiling. The rungs were too narrow for Tav to climb. But his entire body quivered. If he could have leapt to the top of the ladder, he would have.

"Where does that lead?" Andre asked.

"To the roof walk," Elliot answered.

And began, hand over hand, to climb.

Chapter Three

"DON'T WORK TOO hard," Peter said as he kissed Meredith goodbye and swung his leg over his bike. He'd ridden to the Cliff Road house from his cranberry farm that morning. Now that he'd caved to a large white tent and dance floor, as well as six other items George insisted were necessary, he was headed down to Jetties Beach. He was training for a Boston triathlon in October and wanted a long swim in the Sound this afternoon. The water temperature was finally warm enough after a brisk June.

Merry hugged George and jumped into her police Explorer. She had a meeting at the station out on Fairgrounds Road, Peter remembered. But as he pedaled away, he saw that she was frowning, her eyes fixed on the radio near her console. *Somebody on a moped has probably hit a street sign*, he thought. It was constantly happening in high season. He waved goodbye and turned his bike toward town.

A few seconds later, Merry's car roared out in the opposite direction.

THE BODY WAS huddled in a fetal position near an overturned plastic Adirondack chair, a few feet from the roof walk's northern railing. There was little else to be seen on the deck-like space, except a ceramic mug that appeared to have rolled into the walk's far corner, and a cell phone that had long since run out of battery. The corpse might have dropped both *in extremis*. But the mug might just as easily have rolled in a gale of wind. There had been several, Merry thought, since Nora Murphy had gone missing.

More than a month ago, from what the housekeeper said.

Merry stepped gingerly around the perimeter of the roof walk, her shoes covered in a pair of sterile booties. She was waiting for Clarence Strangerfield, who handled forensics for the Nantucket Police, and she didn't want to disturb the scene more than necessary. It had been mauled enough by the man who'd found the body—Elliot Murphy, the victim's brother. She'd glimpsed him briefly on her way upstairs, a nondescript middle-aged man with sandy-colored hair and the mottled skin that so often went with it. He'd been marooned in the living room, drinking straight gin in the company of a friend.

She could tell from disturbances in the roof walk's surface dirt that Elliot had moved quickly across the decking once he'd reached the top of the attic ladder. That was both predictable and forgivable. While one part of his mind must have known that Nora was dead from the moment he saw her, he would have grasped her shoulder and turned her on her back to be sure.

And then screamed.

Nora Murphy's body was badly decayed. It would have bloated a few days after her death, emitting gases as the tissues necrotized, the skin bursting in places. It had been subjected to weeks of wind, sun, and rain. Birds—gulls, probably, which were notorious scavengers—had pecked out the softer parts of the face, including the eyes, and torn at the woman's T-shirt. And then the corpse had started to mummify. The past week had been hot and dry. The hands were shriveled to claws.

Elliot couldn't be sure it was his sister. But the housekeeper, her face twisted with suffering, identified the body. She had laundered the woman's clothes.

From the distance of about a yard, Merry studied the head and huddled frame as well as she could. No obvious wounds. No bloodstains dried and fading on the deck planking. No visible signs of distress in the disposition of the limbs, as there might be if the woman had suffered a seizure of some kind.

And no weapon.

It was a death only the sky had witnessed.

Merry glanced over the rail toward the water lapping Steps Beach far below. The harbor was serene off the Nantucket cliffs. As she watched, a tiny figure knifed through the waves with deliberate strokes, its head seal-dark. She strained her eyes to focus on the flash of water and sunlight: *Peter*. He had no idea she was watching him from this height. The calm precision of his movements connected her isolated and melancholy platform with the normal world in a way that felt almost shocking. Other people were enjoying a summer's day.

She looked back at the corpse. Nora Murphy might simply have lain down to sleep and never awakened. Merry hoped the woman's last moments had been graced with peace and silence. Somehow, she doubted it.

"SHE ARRIVED THE Tuesday before the Wine Festival, and disappeared the following Wednesday, right before Memorial Day weekend," Roseline DaJouste said. Her hands gripped the arms of her chair as she spoke. Her eyes were fixed on an impressionistic oil painting that hung on the opposite wall, a pastel square of boats and wharves and water.

"So she was here roughly a week," Merry said. She had gathered the three inhabitants of the house in the living room while Clarence, along with his two assistants, worked the scene. Howie Seitz was seated at a side table with his laptop open; he was already taking notes.

"She's been here for six," Elliot Murphy broke in. "Roseline only *thought* she'd left."

"I understand, Mr. Murphy. Ms. DaJouste?"

"I get here about ten o'clock in the morning each day and stay until dinner—around five-thirty. Mr. Spence likes it early," the housekeeper said. "I never saw her that Wednesday. I thought she was just out somewhere. Down to the beach, maybe. But the next day her bed still wasn't slept in. Her bath was still clean, like I'd left it. And she didn't come back, all through June."

"It didn't occur to you to file a Missing Person's Report?" Merry asked.

Roseline shook her head. "That is not my place. That would be for Mr. Spencer to do."

"And he wasn't worried when his daughter failed to return?"

"Not much worries him these days." Roseline looked imploringly at Elliot Murphy. "I didn't think to check the roof, Mr. Elliot. Nobody's gone up there for years. I'd have told her it wasn't safe."

"She didn't die from rotting wood," he replied. "It's not your fault, Roseline. The roof walk was one of her special spots when she was little. She used to sit up there and write in her journal. Dad would've had to nail the door shut to keep her out."

"Where is your father?" Merry asked.

Roseline's worried eyes shifted abruptly to the doorway. "He should have been home by now. He was down to the Wharf Rats, miss. Goes there every day. But I never knew him to stay so late before."

So Ralph would certainly be familiar with him, Merry thought. She knew Spencer Murphy's public reputation, which rivaled the late David Halberstam's or Morley Safer's, but she had only seen him from a distance, walking the streets of town. She remembered a wife. One who'd died not long ago.

"That's all we need," Elliot muttered, breaking into her thoughts. "Dad AWOL. Could you put out an APB, Officer, for an elderly man in a Volvo almost as old?"

"Yes," Merry replied, "once you give me a good description of your father, his car, and his license plate. And it's Detective, Mr. Murphy, not Officer."

Elliot lifted his brows in mock apology. He was irritated by her insistence on the point; but she wanted him to be aware of her seniority and take her questions seriously. He was obviously shaken by his gruesome discovery on the roof walk, but he was also strangely cavalier about his sister's death. Shock?

"This whole thing is crazy, Detective," he said, with emphasis on the final word. "I had no idea Nora was even in the country, much less on Nantucket. That she also managed to die, with nobody in the house aware of it, is unbelievable."

"Is it?"

"Of course! Think about it!" His voice rose slightly. "For weeks—*a month*—whatever it is—my dad and Rose-line have been going about their lives, totally unaware that she was rotting up there on the roof! It's like something out of Hitchcock!"

It was probable that Nora Murphy had died of natural causes—an undetected heart ailment or aneurysm, a stroke hitting unexpectedly in relative youth. But Merry could not rule out the possibility of a drug overdose of some kind.

"How old was your sister?"

He closed his eyes in brief calculation. "She was twelve years younger than I am. So that would make her about forty."

"You two don't keep up with birthdays?"

"We don't keep up, period."

Merry digested this. If she could have her brother, Billy, back from the grave, she'd give him a birthday gift every day of the year. "She was considerably younger than you are. There's another sibling, I understand?"

"My brother, David. He's three years older than I am. Nora was adopted just before her fifth birthday, Detective. She came into our lives when I was leaving for college. We never really knew her. She was never really . . . one of us."

"I see. I assume your parents didn't feel that way?"

He shrugged. "It was Dad's decision to take in a half-Lao kid and bring her back here to the States. Mom—I don't really know how Mom felt."

There was a story here, but one Elliot Murphy looked

unready to share. His body had stiffened and his expression was wary.

"Your mother passed away recently?"

"One year, two months, and seven days ago," he said. "Cancer."

And her death, clearly, was far more painful than his sister's would ever be.

"Dad hasn't really been the same since."

"It's been worrying us," his friend offered. "That's partly why we came up here for the Fourth of July weekend. We wanted to check in."

He spoke as though he were family. Merry knew that his name was Andre Henrissaint, that he lived at the same address as Elliot in Manhattan, and had just arrived on-island with him that afternoon. Partners, then? Or married? An interesting pairing, regardless; Elliot was in his early fifties, his sandy hair starting to gray, the most mundane of middle-aged specimens, while Andre looked about fifteen years younger. He was also a foot taller, and might justly be described as beautiful.

"Can you tell me about Nora's health?"

Elliot shrugged. "I never heard there was anything wrong with her. But to be honest, I don't really know. We haven't—*hadn't*—seen each other in about ten years."

Merry felt impatient, suddenly, with his desire to distance himself from this death; it was too much like a shirking of responsibility. Nora Murphy was more than just a casual vagrant who'd died on the roof walk upstairs. "She didn't come to your mother's funeral?"

"No. It took some time to get word to her, actually—we had to track her down through Facebook. By the time she responded, Mother was buried."

"You didn't even have her cell phone number?"

He shook his head.

"When you say you had no idea that she was in the US—where did your sister live, Mr. Murphy?"

"Most recently? Singapore, I think," he said.

"Kuala Lumpur," Andre corrected. "Nora was a freelance journalist, Detective. She wandered pretty widely over the years, primarily in Asia."

"So she followed in her father's footsteps," Merry mused.

"*Adoptive* father," Elliot said. His lips compressed with frustrated contempt. "Of course she did. She adored Spence. She'd do anything to win his approval."

"So would you. So would David." Andre's voice was soft but slightly reproving. "You've tried all your lives to be the one he loves best."

"Pathetic, right?" Elliot lifted his palms in capitulation. "But Nora really was the worst. She was intensely competitive. She told me once that she was glad Dave and I were so much older—because she could pretend she was an only child."

"What did you think of her, Mr. Henrissaint?" Merry asked.

"I never officially met her." Andre turned his remarkable eyes—almost as green as her own—on Merry. "Elliot and I have been together seven years. She hadn't come back during that time."

That you know of, Merry thought.

"Ms. DaJouste," she said, "how did Nora seem to you? Was she healthy? Happy?"

"She needed fattening up." Roseline's mouth curled downward. "Just a tiny little woman, Miss Nora. But polite. And so good to her father. She told him about her adventures, the two of them out in the lawn chairs all day long. And she cooked for him. Asian things. Mr. Spence liked Nora's food."

"What about her mood?" Merry persisted.

"Unsettled," Roseline replied after a moment. "When I asked her how long she planned to stay, she didn't know. Maybe months, maybe days."

"I'm surprised some editor hasn't been trying to find her," Andre observed.

"One may be," Merry said. "We can't know. Her computer's shut down and her phone battery has been dead for a while."

Merry had placed both in evidence bags; she would be setting one of the technically savvy officers on the task of circumventing their passwords.

"Miss Nora was done with reporting." Roseline waved a hand in abrupt dismissal. "She told me she wanted to write a book. She thought she might stay here, on Nantucket, and look after Mr. Spence while she worked on it."

"Did David know that?" Elliot demanded. "He'd have had a pretty strong opinion about Nora moving in."

"Why?" Merry asked.

There was a slight pause. "Let's just say that he's never trusted her farther than he could throw her."

Surprisingly harsh words, with the woman lying like a dried husk upstairs.

Merry glanced at Roseline. "Has David Murphy visited this house in the past six weeks?"

"No, miss."

"Did he know that his sister was here?"

The housekeeper shrugged. "You'll have to ask Mr. Spence."

"It doesn't matter," Elliot broke in impatiently. "David's in Boston. Nora's here. *Dead.* She must have been on something. Drugs of some kind. It's obviously an overdose."

"There are no medications in her bathroom," Merry pointed out. "No recreational drugs that we've found, as yet, although we haven't gone over the entire house. Did she have a history of drug abuse?"

"Not that I know of. But then again, I know nothing about her anymore, right? Roseline? Was she taking something?"

"I never saw that. Just her cigarettes." The housekeeper's voice was stubborn; she had obviously liked Miss Nora.

"Even so." Elliot was talking to Andre now. "That is *so* completely Nora—to come back here just to kill herself. Force us all to notice."

"Except you didn't," Merry said. "Notice."

"And if that's what she wanted," Andre added quietly, "all she had to do was jump off that roof walk."

His logic was so clear that not even Elliot could argue.

"I assume she didn't leave any kind of note, that day you noticed she was gone?" Merry asked.

Roseline shook her head. "Just laundry. I washed and folded it and put it back in her closet."

"Did Mr. Murphy ever ask you where his daughter was?"

"After a few days, miss, he couldn't remember she'd even been here."

"Dad's mind is a sieve," Elliot said. "Hence the request for an APB."

"Then why is he still driving?" Merry asked.

"Because he's Spencer Murphy! *You* try to take a car away from the man who risked his life in war zones all over the world! It ain't gonna happen, Detective. He'd rather die first."

And now he's lost, she thought. *And his daughter's been rotting on the roof for a month.*

"Seitz," she said over her shoulder, "take down the pertinent details on Mr. Murphy's car and send out that APB, will you? And, Elliot, I need your brother's contact information."

Chapter Four

THE EMTs CARRIED the black body bag carefully
down the main staircase. A woman Merry guessed to be
about her own age—middle thirties—followed them. Her
dark hair was neatly caught up at the back of her head
and covered with a plastic shower cap; her clothes were
hidden by a sterile jumpsuit. She held a plastic evidence
bag in gloved hands. Inside the bag was a ceramic mug—
Nora Murphy's.

"You're Detective Folger?" she asked, halting at the
foot of the stairs.

"Yes. And you are?"

"Summer Hughes. I didn't introduce myself when I
arrived, just went straight up to find Clarence Strangerfield. I'm covering for Dr. Fairborn while he's off-island."

Fairborn was a general practitioner who also served as
the Nantucket Police medical examiner in cases of unex-
plained death.

"He left town before the Fourth of July?" Merry said in
disbelief. "Has he told you what you're in for?"

"Nobadeer Beach," Hughes said. "I gather it's pretty
epic."

"That's one word. A sand-coated symphony of blood,
urine, and vomit describes it best. We've hired backup

from the mainland this year, and we're going to try to pinch off alcohol supplies at checkpoints, but it's a problem of sheer numbers. Even fifty of us can't control seven thousand of them."

"I thought it was against the law to drink on the beach."

"It is," Merry agreed. "But oddly enough, it's legal to carry unopened containers *onto* the beach. Go figure. I'm so sorry Fairborn left you holding the bag."

"As it were." The doctor glanced through the open front door; it offered a view of the EMTs as they loaded their black-covered burden into the ambulance. "At least we got this out of the way before the holiday really hit."

"Yes. Thank you for responding. Are you in private practice, or . . . ?"

"I'm on a yearlong rotation. I've been here since January. I'm actually an oncologist with Mass Gen."

Merry knew that Massachusetts General had an oncology program at Cottage Hospital. She'd never had a reason to consult it. "Any thoughts on cause of death?"

"Are you kidding me?" Summer's dark eyes widened. "I wouldn't know where to begin. I've never seen a corpse that decomposed."

"Neither have I."

"I'm sure you noticed that there's no obvious wound or sign of violence," she added. "I'm tempted to call it natural causes—but that doesn't tell us much. We'll have to wait for the autopsy and pathology reports. Toxicology. It could always be an overdose."

"No drugs on the scene," Merry said. "Or in the bedroom."

"Clarence hasn't searched the entire house yet. And by this time, we won't be able to find needle marks on the skin. But the stomach contents may tell us something." Summer lifted the bag in her hands. "I'm sending this mug to Bourne with the body. There's a residue in the bottom that's probably coffee, but it can't hurt to analyze it."

"Right. Thanks."

Bourne, just over the Sagamore Bridge on Cape Cod, was the nearest coroner's office. The corpse would have to be flown there by helicopter. Then it could take weeks to get the toxicology reports from the state crime lab.

Merry gave the doctor her card. "I really appreciate you showing up. Call me if there's anything you need."

"I will." Summer looked from the card to Merry. "I'd love to have coffee sometime, actually. Hear about your work."

"You would?"

"It's been a little hard to meet people on the island. It's so isolated during the winter. And now that it's high season—"

"There are too *many* people." Merry laughed. "I get it. For the next three months you won't have a minute to sit down at Cottage Hospital."

How long had it been since she'd taken the time to get to know a stranger? Half the people on Nantucket were familiar from childhood—and the other half viewed her as an authority figure, best given a wide berth. It would be nice, Merry thought, to spend an hour with another professional woman. Make a friend.

She followed Summer out the door to the drive. The

doctor climbed into the ambulance; she would accompany the body to the Cottage Hospital morgue, where it would lie until its transfer to Bourne. Merry made a mental note to call ahead and request that the medevac flight be delayed until Spencer Murphy was found. He might want to see his daughter's body.

"You missed the staff meeting, Detective."

Bob Pocock's voice caught Meredith just before she reached her office. She'd been hoping he'd have his door closed—he usually did—but she realized he'd been waiting for her. Meetings were Pocock's passion. Missing them was insubordination.

She pulled up in front of his desk. "I'm sorry, sir. I was dispatched to a suspicious death an hour and a half ago."

"And?"

"Forty-year-old woman found in her family home, no sign of violence, could be overdose, could be natural causes. We'll have to await the autopsy."

"Strangerfield show up?"

"Yes, sir. He and his team are still engaged in evidence collection at the scene."

"I want your report by the end of the day."

"Yes, sir."

Pocock looked back at his computer screen; this was all the dismissal Merry could expect. She turned away.

"And, Detective?"

He loved to wait until she'd assumed she could leave, then throw something else at her.

"Yes, sir?"

"From now on, I expect you to take lunch at your desk. No more hours wandering around the island on your own brief. That kind of slack may have been tolerated when your father was chief, but no longer. Understood?"

All too well. "Yes, sir."

"And notify me when you plan to miss a meeting. That's a common courtesy I'm surprised you haven't mastered by now."

"Yes, sir."

She stared straight at his bowed head for the next twenty-eight seconds. Finally, without bothering to make eye contact, Pocock said, "You can go."

THE NANTUCKET TOWN manager had issued a job description for chief of police when the search for John Folger's successor began more than six months before.

Candidate must have received a bachelor's degree in criminal justice or business management. Graduation from a police academy is required. A master's degree in police or public administration, criminal justice, or a related field is preferred. Ten years of experience as a certified police officer, five of which have been in a supervisory capacity, are mandatory.

The notice concluded with instructions for online submission of résumés and references, along with salary information. But Meredith hadn't read that far. Gone were the days when the Folgers handed down the post of chief from generation to generation. When John had succeeded Ralph Waldo two decades before, the townspeople had been comforted by the promise of family continuity and tradition. But Merry knew that the Nantucket Police Department was a different force from the one her father had inherited—partly because of the effort he'd made to modernize its training and facilities. It was as shiny as its new station out on Fairgrounds Road; and Merry figured it was time for new blood at the top. Off-island blood.

She volunteered her opinion defiantly one winter night in her childhood kitchen, although neither Ralph nor John had asked why she failed to apply for her father's vacancy. Merry wanted to nip their speculation in the bud. She would never get the job anyway. She wasn't qualified.

Although she had spent nearly ten years in police work on and off the island, she had too little experience as a supervisor. Howie Seitz was more of a friend than a subordinate. Clarence Strangerfield was a surrogate uncle who'd taught her more than she would ever teach him. And she had no B.A., much less a master's—just an associate degree in criminal justice from Cape Cod Community College. She'd promised herself she'd try to earn a bachelor's online through UMass during the off-season, but planning her wedding had taken precedence.

And if she were brutally honest, she was having doubts about her career altogether. The prospect of relaxing into Peter Mason's life—of raising children on his farm instead of fingerprints at a crime scene—was bewitching. Never since the age of sixteen had she been offered the choice *not* to work.

What would she do with herself if she were free?

Travel, she thought. *See the world. Learn a language. Sleep late on a weekday. Try to cook something edible.*

That might be enough to fill her first six months of marriage. But what then? Would she grow bored? Or worse yet . . . *boring*?

You could go back to school full time. said a voice in her head. *At a four-year college.*

The idea was so disruptive and dangerous—would she really leave Nantucket and Peter for *school?*—that she thrust it immediately out of her mind.

She had a report for Pocock to draft, before the chief left for the day.

Merry's new boss was the result of several months' intensive search on the part of the town manager, who had interviewed more than a dozen candidates. Many were officers who had risen through the ranks in various police departments around New England, who were looking for a capstone to modest careers. They ranged in age from mid-forties to mid-fifties. Pocock was forty-eight years old. But that was where any similarities to his rivals ended. Pocock was a rising law enforcement star. His last job title had been Deputy Chief of the Special Investigative Group of the Bureau of Detectives of the Chicago Police Department.

Merry had pulled up an organizational chart of the CPD when the new chief's hiring was announced, wondering what exactly that series of titles on his résumé meant. She understood immediately that he was a manager and shaper of hundreds of lives. The Special Investigative Group was a huge umbrella unit within the Chicago Police Department. It governed all investigations throughout the city's precincts: property crimes, violent crimes, arson, financial crimes, fugitive apprehension, youth intervention. It supervised a joint task force with the FBI, crime scene processing, and forensics. And Pocock had been second in command.

"What the hell is he doing here?" Merry murmured, as she read the *Inky Mirror*'s profile of the new chief. The newspaper provided few clues. And three months after Bob Pocock was sworn in on a blustery March afternoon, Merry was still no wiser. He was vastly overqualified for, and under-utilized in, his new position. The Nantucket Police Department offered no scope for the sort of ambition and success his career suggested. Setting the budget limits and workday culture of a small group of employees, responsible for the safety of roughly ten thousand year-round residents, with a brief spike up to seventy thousand in July and August, could hardly equal the challenge and vicious survival politics of policing a city of three million.

Pocock, Merry suspected, was on the run from something. He had gone to ground on an island thirty miles out at sea to keep from killing himself.

She had no proof of this, of course. The new chief never fraternized with his subordinates. He only spoke to impose his orders or solicit intelligence regarding ongoing police matters. He never inquired about his officers' or detectives' personal lives. He never asked where he could get a good beer. If he had family or friends from the past, no one knew about them.

Pocock made it clear he thought the department had been poorly managed and that its personnel could improve considerably in their professionalism. He never praised anyone's performance. They were all on notice, Merry knew. Nobody's job was secure. Particularly that of his predecessor's daughter. Maybe if she missed a few more meetings—and neglected to inform her chief—he'd pack her off to a life of leisure at Mason Farms.

Before she could consider this, Howie Seitz stuck his head in her doorway.

"Hey, Mer," he said. "They've found the old guy's car."

Chapter Five

SPENCER MURPHY'S VOLVO was in fairly good condition for a car that had been exposed to salt air for fifteen years. Merry walked around it, noting scratches along both the driver and passenger sides—probably from the untrimmed hedges that lined the entry to Step Above—and a shallow impression in the bumper near the tailpipe. He'd backed into something fairly recently. The car was parked in a shaded spot along New Whale Street and there was a ticket on the windshield. It was a two-hour zone, and Murphy's car had overstayed its welcome by about six. Murphy himself was nowhere to be seen.

"This is a good place to dump your car if you're catching a ferry to the mainland," Howie pointed out.

"If you want a parking ticket on July Fourth weekend." Merry pulled on a latex glove and tried the door handle; unlocked. She glanced inside. A stained coffee mug, a couple of used tissues wadded in the cupholder, and a yellow reporter's notebook tucked on the passenger seat. She flipped it open carefully in case Murphy had left a note. But in page after page of jottings, there was a common thread: he recorded bird sightings, some of them with charming pencil sketches; and he wrote careful instructions to himself, organized by day. Lists of things he needed from the store. Reminders to call people, meet people, remember their names. She had stumbled on Spencer Murphy's vast cheat sheet. He knew he was losing his memory, and he was fighting it.

Under today's date there was only one notation:

Wharf Rats, noon.

"You think he realized we'd figured out he killed his daughter and skipped town?" Howie asked.

"No. I think he's old and lost. Go back to my car and put out a second APB—with just Murphy's description this time. He's probably wandering on foot. Unless he somehow made it home."

She drew her cell phone from her purse and called Clarence Strangerfield. She buzzed him twice before he picked up.

"Hey. Are you done at the house?"

"Half an hour ago," Clarence said cautiously. There was the sound of laughter and a shrieking child in the background.

"Where are you?"

"Something Natural. I was a bit puckish, Marradith, and the cheese-and-chutney on whole grain was calling me."

"Pocock will be calling you next. He wants us to eat at our desks. Find anything after I left?"

"Lots. There are over a dozen rooms in that house. And only one woman to clean them. You don't want to know what's undah the beds."

"Controlled substances, Clare," she said patiently. "Prescription or non. Did you get anything?"

"Just a hahf-empty bottle of a common statin med. Spencer Murphy has high cholesterol, appahrently."

"Is that something we should ask the coroner to test for?"

"It wouldn't kill the girl, Marradith, unless she'd eaten the whole bottle. And even then, it would take a while. She'd die of livah failure over a period of days. Not while she was watching the sunrise."

"Tell the folks in Bourne about it, just the same."

"Ahready did," Clarence said comfortably. "Did you find her father?"

"No. He didn't wander home on foot?"

"He did naht."

"How much of your sandwich is left?"

"I only got a hahf. You know how large they are."

"Can you meet me on New Whale Street, Clarence?"

ANDRE LIFTED THE glasses from the living room table and carried them across the center hall to the side passage that led to the kitchen. Like those in most old, unrenovated houses, it was a small galley space with few windows, a dark linoleum floor, and wood cabinets scuffed with use. The few pots and pans Roseline used to cook the simple meals she gave Spencer Murphy were shining and clean, but they dated to the 1970s. So did the dishes. Even the pot holders by the electric range were gray with time and use.

Andre knew that if Elliot had his way, the room would be tripled in size by folding it into the connecting passage and adjacent study. It would be opened to the rear terrace and filled with light. The cabinets would be white, the floors flagged with limestone, which suited a house by the sea. Elliot would dot the room with his collection of sea-colored glass vessels, handblown by artist friends.

He would cook healthy food on a gas stove under a vent hood encased in stainless steel. The room would strike a razor-edge balance between comforting nostalgia and hip modernity.

Andre was less obsessed with places and things than his partner. He spent his days with people who had so little that his own life seemed inordinately blessed. He was a psychologist who worked with homeless children at shelters in the Bronx. He and Elliot had met at a Designer Show House in Brooklyn; proceeds from the event bene-fited Andre's organization. Elliot had toured him through the place, his enthusiasm for design infectious; it was a window on his skills as a high-end Manhattan realtor. Andre had turned the tables, however, by asking Elliot to help find low-cost buildings in fringe areas that his orga-nization could refurbish and lease. In the past seven years, he and Andre had turned around eight buildings as fresh new shelters for abused women and homeless kids. In the process, they had become friends, lovers, and partners in every sense of the word. Their condo perched above the High Line was an oasis of calm from the stress of both their lives.

He rinsed the empty glasses, soaped them carefully— they were Elliot's mother's old Waterford highballs—and upended them in a rack to dry. He knew Elliot was out-side, standing in the long grass at the end of the garden, staring at the darkening Sound.

Roseline had gone home. Spencer Murphy had not returned. They were alone in the house. With Nora's ghost.

He walked through the hazy, unlit rooms to the French doors and strode across the lawn.

"They found the car," Elliot said. "But not Dad. I just heard."

"They're still looking?"

"Oh, yeah. What if he got on a boat? And ended up in Hyannis? With no idea why he was there—or where *there* was—or how to get back?"

"He'd ask somebody," Andre said. He put his arms around Elliot's waist and drew him close. Elliot's head came up to his chin, no higher, like a child's. Elliot sighed, also like a child, and leaned into Andre.

"I'm sorry," he said. "That this happened. It's ruined our holiday."

"We could go eat," Andre suggested reasonably.

"How can I eat, when my father's . . . out there, somewhere, and Nora's . . ."

"You're not helping Spence by standing here."

Elliot gazed out over the moor shrubs and wild brush that tangled the gulley between the cliff and the farther dunes. "What if he's . . . *down there*, Andre? A corpse like Nora? Covered by the leaves and the vines and the *rugosa* canes . . . lying under the stairs . . ."

"MacTavish would have found him." Andre released Elliot. "Tav didn't smell a thing but seaweed and dead crabs. And he's already had his dinner and gone to sleep on our bed. Now, come on, El. You're making yourself crazy here."

"I can't eat until I call David," he said.

LANEY MURPHY SLIPPED an electrolyte supplement into her water bottle and waited for it to dissolve, shaking it gently, while she unrolled her yoga mat and draped it over her shower door to dry. The basement apartment of her father's old brownstone on Beacon Hill was low-ceilinged and dimly lit, but the bathroom, like the rest of the space, was recently renovated and shone with a marble chill. David Murphy was fastidious. He'd won their longtime cleaning lady when he'd divorced Laney's mother and doubled the woman's working hours. Since moving back in with her dad four months before, Laney had learned to keep her chaotic life shut tightly in her bedroom. She never left a stray flip-flop or hair band anywhere in the rooms upstairs, which her father had arranged like a museum: discreet picture lights beaming gently on the framed art that lined the walls, chairs precisely positioned around low tables boasting a single potted succulent, a single magazine. There was nothing at all on the long, pale gray quartz kitchen counters. Curious, Laney had opened the oven door one night after her father was safely in bed, and scanned the inside. Just as she thought: it had never been used. He had torn out the old kitchen when her mother left, replaced everything down to the last spoon, and then metaphorically turned off the lights. The house seemed sterile without the odors of garlic and lemon, rosemary and lamb, chocolate and raspberry. The only thing David ever made was coffee, in a gleaming new machine piped into the wall that ground its own beans and steamed its own milk. Laney had not yet mastered it and never would; she preferred green tea.

She pulled a sweatshirt over her head, thrust her feet into a pair of sheepskin-lined slippers, and ran lightly up the stairs to the empty kitchen. It was half-lit, like the rest of the rooms, when most of the gorgeous old houses on Charles Street were glowing with lamplight and conviviality. The drinks hour, Mom always called it, as she poured herself a glass of wine and scooped a handful of cashews from the pantry. The ritual signaled the end of the work or school day when Laney was little, the shift to indoor warmth and comfort after the grittiness of daily life in Boston, like throwing a match on the fire in winter or slipping into a hot bath when her muscles ached. Comfort had leached out of her father's house when Mom left. Laney thought of her now, pouring a similar drink, probably, in her studio in Brooklyn—but alone. Or maybe not: Mom had a genius for making friends. Maybe she was sitting with one at a tiny table in a trendy neighborhood bar, her gray hair sliding from behind her ears, laughing.

She had invited Laney to move in with her when the teaching job had turned out to be unbearable and her work as a yoga instructor failed to pay the rent. But Laney knew how small the studio was. She'd be sleeping on a pullout couch and folding it back up every morning. There was nowhere to store her clothes. She'd have no privacy. Neither would Mom. She winced at the thought of her mother bringing a stranger back to her bed at night—that was totally mind-blowing and uncomfortable to envision—but all the same, she didn't want to invade Mom's freedom. Kate had spent enough years taking care of Laney as it was. And then there was Dad—

Dad, who had retreated even further into himself now that Mom was gone. Whose fluorescent pallor, under his close-cut cap of silver hair, suggested a life lived behind bars.

She opened the refrigerator door; the empty whiteness stared back at her. Scrupulously clean shelves. A stick of butter and a bottle of dressing on the door, a bag of coffee beans, three limes, and a liter of vodka. Yesterday's paper carton of Thai takeout sat in splendid isolation on the top glass shelf. She opened the vegetable drawer and drew out the baby greens and avocado, the block of Parmesan and the quinoa she'd bought a few days ago. Hesitant to violate the oven with fat-splattering protein, she lived on salad now. And the occasional pizza Rory gave her when she slept over at his place.

She grated the Parmesan with a vegetable peeler, drizzled the greens with champagne vinaigrette, and cubed the avocado. The quinoa had currants in it. She opened a can of water-packed tuna and flaked it carefully with a fork over the salad, then rinsed the can so it wouldn't smell in the trash and offend her father. Before she left the kitchen, she wiped the counter clean. Laney's whole life was a tug-of-war between her mother's rich appetites and her dad's asceticism.

There was a light under his office door; working late again. No sound of keyboard or soft rumble of conversation, however. No TV. She grasped her metal bowl in one hand and padded in her slippers down the hall. Hesitating for a fraction of a second, she rapped her knuckles against the mahogany door. It was ajar. When he didn't answer, she opened it slightly and inserted just the right half of her face into the room.

Her father was staring straight ahead, one arm of his reading glasses dangling from the corner of his mouth. His eyes shifted slowly to hers, but no expression crossed his face, no hint of welcome or even recognition. After a second, he said: "Sit down."

She came around the door and slid quietly into the

chair in front of his desk. She set her salad bowl on the floor beside her. "You okay?"

"I'm fine. Your aunt has been found dead in the Nantucket house and your grandfather is missing. Can you take a few days off?"

"From the studio? Of course, but—"

"Elliot has asked me to come. There will have to be a funeral."

"For Grandpa Spence?" she stuttered, bewildered.

"For your *aunt*. Pack for three days. We'll leave for Logan at eight A.M. Don't oversleep."

He rose from his desk and walked out of the room without another word.

Laney listened to him mount the stairs to the upper floor, the rooms she never entered now. Her heart was beating wildly. The smell of tuna drifted to her nostrils, bringing bile into her throat.

"What aunt?" she whispered.

JODIE JAMESON STEPPED out the back service door of American Seasons and dipped his cigarette to the match flaring between his hands. Then he lifted his head and let a spiral of smoke drift into the night air. It had been humid earlier, the restaurant kitchen like a frantic sauna, all the line workers shining with sweat, but now there was a slight wind rippling through the streets of Nantucket. Jodie glimpsed a few stars. A few clouds scudded over the moon. The weather was shifting. It would be bright and clear tomorrow.

The restaurant had fronted Centre Street for decades, but here at the rear of the building, all was deep night, the darkness beneath sheltering tree branches, and relative quiet. Jodie was sous-chef at American Seasons. Regulars had booked their tables months ago for this first night of July Fourth weekend and he was feeling the effects of a long day. He pulled out his phone and glanced at the time: twelve minutes past ten. Table service was done, but the bar would be open another two hours. His thirty-second break was over. He inhaled deeply and dropped his smoke beneath his kitchen clog.

Which was when the old man's face suddenly loomed out of the trees, wavering as he shuffled toward Jodie. The cook squinted, peering beyond the back-door spotlight. "Can I help you?"

"The jungle's too quiet. They're waiting with their knives." Spence Murphy held out his cigarette. "Gotta light, soldier?"

Chapter Six

MERRY WAS DRINKING café au lait in Peter's bed
when Howie texted her the next morning. She was supposed to watch the Firecracker 5K—a July Fourth sprint
along Monomoy for Peter and several hundred other
early-risers. Forty-five minutes later she pulled up at
Spencer Murphy's house instead.

Andre Henrissaint met her at the door.

"He's lying down in his room, but he's not sleeping,"
he said. "Elliot's sitting with him."

"He came home last night, I understand?"

"Around ten-thirty." Andre shrugged slightly.
"He turned up at American Seasons. They said he
was hallucinating—reliving his escape from Laos, I
think. He couldn't remember how to get home, but
he remembered this address, oddly enough. So they
gave him a drink and an order of duck breast to go,
and put him in a taxi."

"The mind is a strange thing."

"Very. I say that, and I'm trained as a psychologist."

"Have you told Mr. Murphy about his daughter?"

"Several times. He forgets."

Merry followed Andre to Spence Murphy's bedroom,
which was on the main floor. More reason, she thought,

that Nora's body had gone undetected on the roof—once she disappeared and her room was tidied, neither her father nor his housekeeper had any reason to go upstairs. They resumed their habits of living among a few hundred square feet of the enormous old house: kitchen, bedroom, bath, and the small den Merry glimpsed through a doorway, lined with bookshelves and littered with photographs from Murphy's reporting days. Nora had been undisturbed in her open-air tomb.

Andre paused in the doorway.

Spencer Murphy's bedroom had once been something else—a sunporch in the 1950s, maybe—and only recently converted to a main-floor master bedroom as its owner's balance and strength grew weaker. What had once been screened panels were now glass, lined with floor-to-ceiling drapes. French doors similar to the living room's led out to the back deck. An adjoining powder room had been converted with a drop-in stall shower. There was a spectacular view of the harbor.

Elliot was seated in a wing chair near his father's bed, a mug of coffee balanced on his knee. The look of bewildered strain Merry had last registered on his face was gone. He seemed placid this morning and, if anything, bored.

"He's bringing *Laney*," he was saying to his father. "Not Kate. Kate doesn't live with them anymore."

"Why not?" Spencer Murphy asked. He hadn't seemed to notice Andre standing in the doorway.

"They're divorced, Dad."

"Since when?"

"A year ago. Remember—you knew this at Mom's funeral. I'm putting Laney in Mom's old sewing room."

"Can't she sleep with her parents? We could set up the crib."

"Not at her age."

"A cot, then. She'll have nightmares if she's alone."

"Dad, she's twenty-four years old. She doesn't want to sleep with either of her parents."

Elliot glanced in exasperation at the doorway, saw Merry behind Andre, and set down his mug. "Detective Folger. Good morning. He found his way home, as you can see."

"Who did?" Spencer Murphy demanded. He lifted his chin pugnaciously. "That Negro doesn't live here. I've never seen him before in my life."

There was a hideous silence. Merry felt her face flush with shock and embarrassment. She glanced at the man standing rigidly beside her. Then he turned and left.

"Andre—" Elliot surged after him. "Dad—"

"Go," Merry murmured. "I'll stay with your father."

She walked over to the bedside and offered her hand to Spencer Murphy. "Good morning, sir. I'm Meredith Folger. With the Nantucket Police. I understand you got a little lost yesterday."

He grasped her fingers politely. "Then you understand wrong, young lady. I was right here at home all day."

"I see. We were a little worried, sir, because we found your car down on New Whale Street."

The brown eyes, dimmed with the gray film of age, flickered slightly. "Must have left it there. I'll pick it up later."

"Yes, sir. How are you feeling this morning?"

"All right. How are you?"

"I'm well. Could I ask you a few questions?"

"If you like. But I'm usually the one that does the interview."

"I know that, sir." Merry took out her laptop and turned it on.

"I don't use one of those things, though. Never have. Can't type. Barbara does all my typing for me."

Barbara, Merry remembered, was the dead wife's name.

"She's a little tired this morning and asked if I'd take notes," she said.

"I don't mind. What did you say your name was?"

"Folger. I'm with the Nantucket Police."

"Ralph Folger runs the police."

"He's my grandfather, sir."

"Grandfather! Not old enough to be a grandfather. He and Sylvie just have the one boy, yet."

At the sound of her grandmother's name, Merry felt her throat constrict.

"I understand your daughter, Nora, paid you a visit a few weeks ago," she said.

"Nora?" Spence shrugged slightly. "Not here now. Haven't seen Nora in a long time. Had some trouble with Barbara. Took off in a huff. Barbara says we shouldn't worry—she'll be back when she's hungry. Kids that age always are. Say they're running away, and they're back by dinnertime."

"Mr. Murphy, your daughter was staying here in the house a few weeks ago. Do you remember that? She sat outside on the back lawn with you and told you stories? Made you Asian food for dinner?"

"She had a way of doing street noodles, like her mother. Fish sauce and curry. Scallops instead of shrimp."

"Sounds good."

The filmy eyes flickered again. "Nora," he said. "Talking about the old days in Laos. She got me smoking again. Do you have a light?"

"No, sir, I'm afraid I don't. So you remember she was here?"

"I do." He sat a little higher against his bed pillows, his voice suddenly firm. "We had some great talks. She'd been in Southeast Asia. Reporting there. None of the old fellas are still around, of course, but I told her what it was like when I was there. She's part Lao, you know."

The mind, Merry thought, was definitely weird. Spencer Murphy's seemed to flash on and off like a Christmas bulb.

"We found Nora yesterday on the roof walk, Mr. Murphy. Your son Elliot told you that she seems to have died there?"

He closed his eyes, slowly and painfully. He drew a deep breath. "Yes. I remember. *Yes.*"

"Do you have any idea when she went up on the roof?"

"Every day," he said.

"Every day?"

"It's her place. She loves the roof."

"Was she happy while she was here?"

"Of course! Nora loves the island. She's going to stay. Wants to write a book."

"When did you last see her, Mr. Murphy?"

He opened his eyes and looked straight at Merry. "Yesterday?" he asked. "This morning? She's a big girl now. She comes and goes."

MERRY FOUND ANDRE and Elliot in the kitchen. Elliot was rinsing dishes. Andre was pouring coffee beans into the top of an elaborate machine that seemed out of place in the old-fashioned galley. Neither was speaking.

"Was your father physically okay when he returned last night?" Merry asked.

"He was fine," Elliot replied. "Exhausted, but otherwise unharmed. He had absolutely no idea where he'd been all day. He was babbling about jungles and knives. The old Pathet Lao story again." He shook the water off a dish and placed it on the counter. Then he reached for a towel and dried his hands. "My brother, David, is due any minute. He's Dad's executor and power of attorney—we figured it had to be the kid who was physically closest to Nantucket. Dave can get here from Boston in an hour."

"You informed him of Nora's death?"

"Oh, yeah," Elliot said. "But he's really coming because of Dad. I mean, Nora's dead and everything, but who knows when the coroner will release her body? You haven't even flown it to Bourne yet, right?"

"I was waiting for your father to turn up," Merry said. "I thought he might ask to see Nora."

Elliot shook his head. "I don't think he's fully grasped that she's dead. And I doubt he will, under the circumstances. You might ask David about that, once he's here."

"Your father is certainly confused," Merry said. "But his memory seems to shift in and out. He remembered Nora telling him about her reporting life, for instance, but couldn't pinpoint the last time he saw her."

"Does it matter?" Elliot asked. "We know which day she disappeared, from Roseline."

"I was hoping Mr. Murphy could tell me something about Nora's mood in her final days. Her plans, if she had any. This idea of moving in with him to write a book, for instance. His observations might help us figure out if she was unhappy enough to harm herself—or help us to rule that out."

"Suicide."

"Yes," Merry agreed. "We'll have a better idea what killed her once the coroner's report is filed. But in the meantime—if your father happens to remember anything that you think might be relevant, Mr. Murphy, would you write it down?"

"Sure. I'll let you know."

"Would you like some coffee, Detective?" Andre asked.

"I'd love some," Merry said gratefully. She leaned against the counter, watching his deft hands. He had beautiful fingers, long and tapering, with almond-shaped nails.

Andre reached for the bag of beans; almost empty. "I brought this from New York, but we've gone through it quickly. Late nights and early mornings will do that."

"There should be more in the cupboard," Elliot suggested. "Not Dad's percolator stuff, but the beans David got when he gave him the machine."

"You didn't bring that from New York, too?" Merry asked.

"No. It was a Christmas gift. David likes to give people things he wants to use himself. He hates Dad's percolator. Dad, of course, has never learned to use David's machine, which automatically grinds the beans. Dave's a little obsessed with coffee."

"I get it."

"In cases of dementia," Andre said, "one of the first cognitive skills to wane is mastery of the new. Spence was never going to use this machine. But kudos to Dave for trying."

He rummaged in the cupboard to the right of the stove and succeeded in finding a Nantucket Coffee Roasters' bag. "Chester's Blend," he said. "Named after the company dog, apparently." He scooped out some beans. And then frowned.

"Too old?" Elliot asked.

"Maybe. What are these?"

Elliot leaned over Andre's shoulder and stared at the scoop of dark brown beans. So did Merry. Among them were lighter, caramel-colored beans she didn't recognize. "A different roast?" she suggested.

"I don't think that's even coffee," Andre said. "It's more like a seed."

"You can pick them out," Elliot said. "It's still usable."

"I would hope," said a voice from the doorway. "It's a brand-new coffeemaker."

Merry turned.

"David!" Elliot said with relief. "I'm so glad you're here."

The man in the doorway was taller, leaner, and older-looking than Merry expected. But his resemblance to Spencer Murphy was uncanny. She remembered television images of the reporter from two decades before; he might have been this man, brought forward in time. By David Murphy's side was a sturdy-looking young woman with red hair hanging in waves down her back. Her eyes were gray and her skin was dead white, overlaid with Elliot's freckles.

"Hey, Laney," Andre said.

She slipped away from her father and hugged Andre fiercely.

"And who is this?" David asked.

"I'm Detective Meredith Folger," she replied. "Nantucket Police."

He offered his hand. It was cool and dry. "They needed you to make coffee?"

Elliot laughed. "Hardly. She's about to arrest us all for parental neglect."

"We're a little confused." Andre passed David the bag of coffee.

"Chester's Blend. I bought it at Christmas." David sifted through the beans with his fingers. "Somebody's stuck dried apricot seeds in here."

"Apricot seeds?" Merry repeated.

"Yes." His eyes flicked up to meet hers. "They're the dried kernels found inside apricot pits. A trendy snack of my daughter's. Detective, this is DeLaney Murphy."

Merry shook the girl's hand.

"Laney brought the seeds with her to Nantucket. She's the family health nut."

"Not really," the girl said quickly. "I just thought they might help Nana. A year ago, when she was sick. They're supposed to cure cancer."

Her voice drifted to silence on the last word; her expression was miserable.

David set the coffee on the counter. "I guess Dad confused the two. Poor bastard. He's really losing it, isn't he?"

"He lost Nora on the roof for a month," Elliot said.

Laney's eyes widened. *"What?"*

"Never mind." David Murphy was dismissive. "I'd better go talk to him. Is there anything more we can do for you, Detective? I came in for a family conference, as you've probably guessed, and my time is valuable."

"So is mine," she replied, "so I'll be brief. Your sister's remains are in the Nantucket Cottage Hospital morgue, Mr. Murphy. We delayed medevacking them to the coroner in Bourne until your father was found, in the event he wished to see his daughter. Would you like me to delay that transfer any longer, or should we proceed with your sister's autopsy?"

"Proceed," David said.

"Okay. The coroner should release your sister's remains for burial by Tuesday or Wednesday morning. I realize it's a holiday weekend, and you may not be able to plan a funeral immediately, but you should arrange to receive—"

"Can't she just be cremated in Bourne?" Elliot suggested.

"Elliot," Andre said tightly, "if it's her ashes you want returned, you *need to set that up*. And plan a funeral. Spence loved her."

"I'm surprised you can still call him that. After what he called you."

"I know Spence," Andre retorted. "That wasn't him talking, back there. Spence is gone."

"Is there anything else, Detective?" David asked impatiently.

Merry handed him her card. "Until the coroner's report is in, there's little we can do to pinpoint the cause of your sister's death. As for your father—I'd suggest you find his keys, pick up his car on New Whale Street, and make sure he never drives again."

There was a brief silence. "The keys were in his pants pocket," Elliot offered. "I can get the car."

"That's a job for you, Laney," David said. "You'll enjoy the walk into town. *Exercise*."

He turned back into the hall, heading for Spence Murphy's bedroom without another word.

"He can be *such* a prick sometimes," Elliot breathed. "My apologies, Detective. The Murphys are covering themselves in glory this week, aren't they? We'll put it down to grief."

He raised his hand, as though to guide Merry to the front door, but she was already ahead of him.

Grief, she thought, was the very last thing any of the Murphys seemed to feel.

Chapter Seven

THE TIDE WAS going out. Laney's feet were bare and she left deep heel imprints in the hard sand below the seaweed line on Steps Beach. She was moving in a crab-like crouch, turning over the shells with her hands. Most were slipper shells—a type of snail, she thought, or maybe a limpet. Her grandmother used to call them quarterdeck shells, an old-fashioned name, and said they were invasive. She had offered this judgment with her nose slightly wrinkled, as though the slipper snails threatened her privacy. As a result, Laney valued scallop shells more. They were much rarer on Steps Beach, her prize as she scavenged in the sand, one scallop for every fifty slippers. Most of them were empty, but Laney occasionally found live slipper snails, their shells stacked on top of each other in groups of four or five, like nesting teacups.

Groups of sunbathers were scattered about the beach. It was possible some were even neighbors who had descended their own sets of stairs to stake their claims under marine-blue and citrus-colored umbrellas. But Laney doubted it; she didn't know Grandpa's neighbors anymore. His was the last house on Lincoln Circle, right before it became Indian Ave. Many of the other houses on that part of the cliff had changed hands in recent years.

Her father never talked about it, but Uncle Elliot was a realtor and he talked about nothing else. The houses were renovated and expanded with full-height concrete foundations that held exercise gyms and wine cellars and media rooms. The gardens were planted and maintained by local landscape companies and encircled with massive hedges. Their owners might be on-island for the Fourth, but they were hidden behind their walls of green, lounging by their pools, their backs turned to the sea.

Her father, she thought, would be much more comfortable in a house like that—one that could be built anywhere—than he was in his childhood home, musty with emotions and memories. But Laney, like the rest of the Murphys, loved Step Above. The house held everything warm and indelible from her childhood.

Andre splashed out of the shallows toward her. His dark skin gleamed with sun and seawater; his surfer shorts were corded neatly over his flat abdomen. Laney registered both his physical beauty and the fact that it had nothing to do with herself. She trusted Andre more than her father or uncle because he was closer to her own age—and he understood how her mind worked. She had been telling him her innermost thoughts for years.

He reached for a towel and ran it over his body. "You okay in Boston?"

"I guess." Laney dropped her collection of scallop shells back in the sea and let the undertow take them. She dusted grains of sand from her palms. "Although my dad is certifiably weird. Did you know about this sister of his?"

The word *aunt* seemed impossible.

"Yes," Andre said.

"You knew she existed."

"Sure."

"I didn't."

He glanced at her. "Your mom never mentioned Nora? I'm surprised. She wasn't in the habit of editing your childhood."

"I *know*, right?" Laney began to walk beside him, back to the private steps. The sun was hot and she would have liked to go in the water herself, but she needed to discuss this with Andre. "I called her last night. To ask what she knew. I mean, my dad just announces my aunt's dead without ever telling me there's an aunt in the first place? WTF?"

"How is Kate?"

"She's fine. Really good, actually, now that she's left Boston. She said this Nora person was always trying to turn Grandpa Spence against Dad and Uncle El, so they stopped talking to her."

"That's the story I heard."

"Did El tell you anything else?"

He looked away from her, at the sea. "Just that she was adopted during Spence's last trip to Laos—that was after his whole hostage period, around 1980. She's much younger than Elliot and Dave. It sounds like she and the guys just didn't have much in common."

"Neither do you and El. I mean—"

She stopped by the bottom of the stairs, her pale skin flushing an ugly red. "You're younger. And you're—"

"Black," he said.

"—so much *smarter*," she finished.

After an instant, they both laughed. Andre threw his

arm around her shoulder, his palm icy from the sea. They marched deliberately up the stairs. "Have you got any bluefish pâté, Dre?" she asked.

"Have you got any gin, girlfriend?"

"Got any limes?"

"If you've got tonic."

It was an old ritual between them. Laney suddenly felt less orphaned than the day before, less lost than she had in the basement of her father's brownstone. It was high summer in the place she loved best, and MacTavish might even sleep on her bed that night.

But when they mounted the last flight of steps up the cliff, her father was standing in the rose-covered arch. His flat gray eyes were cold with fury.

Laney stopped short. Andre's hand dropped from her shoulder.

"What gave you the right," David asked bitterly, "to invite your *mother* here, miss?"

MERRY PULLED INTO the police station parking lot just as her cell phone trilled. It was the special ringtone she reserved for Peter. She picked up immediately.

"How'd the race go?"

"Fine. Gorgeous day. The police were out in force."

"Community Service Officers," she corrected.

"I know. You brought in a boatload of them." He sounded amused. "I just got a text from Will Starbuck."

Will was the son of Tess Starbuck, the chef and owner of the Greengage restaurant who was catering Merry and Peter's wedding. Will was also the stepson of Peter's farm foreman and close friend, Rafe da Silva.

"Didn't Will run the 5K with you?"

"Nope. He's already out at Nobadeer. Along with about a thousand other kids."

"But it's only July second!" Merry howled.

"I know. That's why I'm calling. Looks like the party's starting early this year."

Cursing, Merry said a hurried goodbye and almost ran into the police station. As a detective, she wasn't technically responsible for the extra patrols and checkpoints the Nantucket Police Department had intended to deploy this year to control the holiday chaos, but she thought the uniformed branch would like to know they'd been neatly sidestepped by about two days.

"Thanks for showing up, Detective."

Pocock was standing just beyond the station's reception desk, surrounded by a group of Community Service Officers. Most of them were strangers. But Howie was discernible among them, in uniform.

"Yes, sir," she said—it was her automatic response to Pocock—and she edged neatly around the group. Howie stared unswervingly at the chief.

"Right," Pocock said. "The *Boston Globe* decided to publish a piece last night telegraphing our punch. They let the world know we intend to shut down this party on the Fourth, and that we're deliberately holding fireworks tomorrow, on the third, to avoid being overcommitted on the holiday. So these asinine kids decided to move the target. They brought the party in early, and used social media to do it. We can expect mayhem, on Nobadeer and elsewhere, for the next three days. I want you all deployed at our checkpoints along the access roads, I want orange barrier fences erected between the dunes and the beach, I want six of you stationed at the airport to keep people from walking or driving onto the sand from the tarmac, and I want you to arrest every single asshole you find underage drinking or shitting in the dunes. Understand? You'll be using disposable plastic handcuffs as restraints, also known as zip ties. You all familiar with them?"

He held up something that looked like a plastic strap for securing baggage tags, double-looped for a pair of wrists. "If we don't have a couple hundred kids booked tonight, you guys aren't doing your jobs. Understand?"

There was a chorus of assent from the assembled CSOs.

"—And no drinking what you confiscate," Pocock added with a touch of sarcasm. "Any officer found to be inebriated will be immediately relieved of his or her duties and sent back to the mainland on the first available ferry."

Merry hastened toward her office. A gaggle of her colleagues were lingering in the back hallway, watching Pocock marshal the troops. She glimpsed the Potts brothers, department veterans, with their hands in their pockets and sullen expressions on their faces. She felt a brief flare of sympathy. She'd heard they were thinking of quitting.

"Now, line up outside in front of the vans," the chief barked. "Uniformed Nantucket police will be transporting you to your specific stations. You will be assigned to teams en route, each team reporting to a designated Nantucket police officer throughout the day. Cases of water will be held on the vans for your relief. You can expect to be on duty until at least six o'clock today and much later tomorrow. Dismissed."

Merry shut her office door and slid into her desk chair

with a sigh of relief. Pocock was efficient, no doubt, and he'd nip the Nobadeer bacchanal in the bud—but he was also grim, and joyless, and his whole take on the holiday threatened to rip the sunshine from the summer day. She wondered if he'd even bother to celebrate the Fourth, or crack a smile—much less a beer. However little her father had liked the destructive force of the pop-up beach party in recent years, he'd taken joy in the rest of Nantucket's July Fourth weekend—because the town's rituals had been part of his childhood, and Ralph's, and Merry's own. That was the difference, she thought, between being born in the community you policed and merely brought in from outside to control it.

For the first time she wondered whether Pocock had cared more for his native Chicago than he did for Nantucket Island—or if every community was the Enemy.

Her desk phone rang.

It was Summer Hughes, from the Cottage Hospital.

"I tried to reach Clarence Strangerfield, but I gather it's his day off," the doctor said.

Merry had a sudden image of Clare's wide bottom suspended over his tomato plants. The forensics chief usually avoided working weekends, and so far Pocock's disapproval had failed to faze him.

"I was just about to call you, Doctor," she said. "The Murphy family has okayed the removal of the cadaver to Bourne. You can send it out anytime."

"That's good to know. I've already heard from them."

"The Murphys?"

"Bourne," Summer corrected. "You know that mug we recovered from the roof? Clarence had me overnight it to the Crime Scene Services Section yesterday."

This was a department of the Massachusetts State Police Crime Lab that processed forensic evidence. If the lab had gotten back to Summer already, there must be news. Merry felt the hairs rise on the back of her neck.

"And?" she said.

"That residue in the bottom of the mug?"

"Coffee?"

"Cut with milk and cyanide," Summer finished.

K ATE　M URPHY　WAS sitting in Step Above's faded living room a few feet from her father-in-law, her hand resting lightly on his wrist as though she were taking his pulse. She had once worked as a registered nurse, and old habits died hard. She had pushed her sunglasses to the crown of her head, securing her thick gray hair behind her ears. She wore khaki shorts and a striped summer blouse, the sleeves rolled to her elbows. Her clothes were a trifle limp—the early breeze had dropped and the air was growing heavy with humidity. Kate's deep blue eyes were bracketed with crow's-feet. Her nose was sharply aquiline. Marionette lines ran from her nostrils to the corners of her mouth, because she smiled widely and often. She was in her early fifties and comfortable, Andre thought, with the face she had earned.

She rose as he walked into the room, her eyes lighting up.

"Andre! Laney! Come here, baby girl!"

Her daughter swooped to hug her—Kate was six inches shorter—and Andre leaned in to kiss her cheek. He glanced at Spence Murphy as he did so, braced for a rebuke. But the old man's expression was warm and open.

In his right mind, Andre thought.

"Where's Elliot?" Spence asked.

"Getting me iced tea," Kate said. "Do you want any?"

"I'm fine. Have a seat, all of you." Spence patted the sofa beside him.

Laney sank down, curling her legs beneath her. "Andre's damp and I'm sandy, Grandpa."

"Glad to hear it. Maybe you two'll give me a hand down the steps later on. I never get to the beach these days."

"Why not?" Kate asked. "Has the weather been bad?"

She had no idea, Andre realized, how vague Spence had become. She'd arrived on one of his good days.

"Too shaky," Spence said. "Those rails need repair. Can't trust 'em."

"Maybe David and El can help. While they're here."

"Neither of them can drive a hammer," Spence said dismissively.

"I can," Andre offered.

The old man's eyes crinkled with amusement. "Of course. You're the son I never had."

That was the familiar Spence: embracing and easy. But he could not be trusted to remain; he would slip away like a ghost as exhaustion crept up on his mind. Andre felt a spiritual pain, aware of the personality they were losing. Had already lost.

Elliot appeared with the iced tea.

"Where's David?" he asked Andre under his breath as he took a chair beside him.

"On the back lawn."

"Hyperventilating?"

"Exactly."

Andre sipped the tea. It had been steeped with loose

Darjeeling and fresh mint Elliot bought from a market in the East Village. It tasted like liquid mahogany.

"You're good to find a room for me, El," Kate was saying. "I realize it was short notice."

"I'm so glad you came," Laney said, "even if Daddy's furious at me."

"Is he?" her mother replied. "Whatever for?"

"Because you aren't welcome here, Kate," David said.

He was observing them from the safe distance of the center hall, which meant he had avoided the obvious path to the living room from the deck. As though he needed to sneak up on them, Andre thought—as though a normal approach would leave him too exposed.

"That's no reason to take it out on Laney," Kate said mildly.

He ignored this. "I would like you to leave as soon as possible."

"Nonsense," Spence said testily. "She's only just arrived."

"Dad." David's voice was very quiet. "She's not my wife anymore. She *left me*. She left Laney. She has no right—"

"To exist?" he retorted. "Good God, you're like your mother, David. You can't let go of a wound, can you? Just keep pulling off the scab, over and over, so it never heals. Kate is my guest. She can stay as long as she likes."

He placed his hand over his daughter-in-law's and squeezed it briefly. "You were the only one who liked Nora anyway," he said. "I'm glad you'll be here for the funeral."

There was a tense silence. Andre saw David's face suffuse with color, then fade to dead white. Anger, violently suppressed. It could not be healthy for a man to suppress so much.

They all listened as he mounted the worn stairs, one foot deliberately in front of the other.

"Then that's settled," Kate said. "Shall I just share Laney's room? And how about some lunch?"

Chapter Eight

"CYANIDE POISONING IS hardly accidental," Bob Pocock said.

"With respect, sir, I'd like to assess the evidence before I determine that."

Merry was standing in front of the chief's desk, as usual. He never invited anyone to sit down, although he had two black leather conference chairs in the room. She had helped her father choose them, two years ago. She was surprised they hadn't been thrown out along with John Folger's secretary.

Pocock raised his eyebrows. "Go ahead. But you'll figure out eventually that it was suicide or murder. That leaves few possibilities. Either the father killed her, or the housekeeper did. Know yet what kind of cyanide it was? Hydrogen? Potassium? Sodium?"

"No, sir. I'm going to pick up the lab report on my way to the family house."

"She either inhaled it or ingested it," Pocock said impatiently. "Given that the residue was found in her coffee cup, obviously she ingested it. Hydrogen cyanide is a *gas*. You clearly didn't know that, Detective, which surprises me; I'd expect you to have researched the poison before you walked into this office. But never mind. I've narrowed the possibilities for you. It was sodium cyanide or potassium cyanide."

"Thank you, sir." Merry's expression was wooden. "I would point out, however, that hydrogen cyanide can also be found in liquid form. Sodium and potassium cyanide are powders, and obviously could have been dissolved in the coffee. All three are inorganic. However, a fourth form of the poison exists—*organic* cyanide. It's naturally produced by some bacteria, algae, fungi, and plants. The victim's contact with it could therefore have been accidental."

"Not if it was in her coffee," Pocock countered. "You can't get around the cup. Either she put it there, or someone else did. And as there were only two other people in the house at the time, Detective, this should be an open-and-shut case. Am I wrong?"

"I would never suggest that, sir."

Pocock locked eyes. If he caught the mocking undertone to Merry's words, he chose not to betray it. "Good. I don't want to hear about this case again until the Fourth of July is over. But Tuesday morning, Detective, I expect charges. And a case to back them up."

"I'll do my best, sir."

"Your best better be good enough."

There was no possible reply to this. Merry counted slowly in her head until, at thirty-three seconds, the chief said, "You can go."

NANTUCKET COTTAGE HOSPITAL sat on a wedge of land between Prospect Street and Vesper Lane, where the historic houses that lined the irregular streets sloping down from Mill Hill met the commercial edge of town.

Summer Hughes could have scanned the lab report from Bourne straight into Merry's inbox, but Merry had asked if she could spare fifteen minutes to talk—and the doctor had agreed.

The waiting room was filled with the usual casualties of a Nantucket holiday weekend: cobblestone rash from bike-riders who'd fallen at high speed on the bumpy streets; lacerations from moped accidents; a few kids who looked drunk but had somehow escaped the police cordon and arrest. One of these, dressed only in a stars-and-stripes bikini, had her head between her knees and was heaving gently. Merry looked away.

Summer met her at the reception desk and led her back to a small, windowless examination room. The doctor took a rolling stool near her computer; Merry sat in the chair reserved for patients.

"A copy of this report should be in Clarence Stranger-field's email," Summer said, "but the lab called me, too, as my contact info was on both the cadaver and the mug paperwork."

Merry scanned the sheet Summer handed her.

"This says she was poisoned by a nitrile, not cyanide."

"Nitriles are compounds of the cyan group and a carbon group. Also known as organic cyanides," the doctor explained.

"Ah."

"I was surprised it was a nitrile—I assumed Nora Murphy was poisoned by hydrocyanic acid. That's a common ingredient in pesticides and some rat fumigation products."

"Which, in a house as old as Step Above, could just conceivably be lying around," Merry mused.

"Right. I thought she might have seen the fumigant in the garage or attic, decided to commit suicide, and put it in her coffee. But from this report, I'm clearly wrong. Still, it's weird, Merry—organic cyanides exist, but they're less toxic and the body *can* metabolize them. I don't understand how she ingested enough to kill her."

"I did some research." Merry set the report down on Summer's examination table. "Organic cyanide is found in bacteria and algae and some tropical plants, like bamboo and manioc—none of which jumped into Nora's coffee cup in a high enough concentration to poison her. But it's also found in the pits of stone fruit."

"Cherries and almonds," Summer said. "In all the Agatha Christie books, the victim smells bitter almonds right before he collapses over his cocktail glass."

"Not to mention bitter apricots," Merry said. "A health nut recently told me that the dried seeds cure cancer. You're an oncologist, Summer. Is that a totally bogus claim?"

"Pretty much. But when you're desperately ill, you'll try anything. The nitrile in bitter apricot seeds is called amygdalin, or sometimes laetrile. It's banned in the US partly because of the cyanide danger. But people used to go to Mexico to get it—" Summer's brown eyes suddenly widened. "Oh, shit. Was Nora Murphy a health nut?"

"I don't know," Merry replied. "But there were dried apricot seeds in the cupboard. Dried apricot seeds mixed up in a bag of coffee beans I'm betting she used. And Nora's mother died over a year ago of cancer."

"Send some of those seeds to Bourne," Summer said, "for comparison with the residue in Nora's coffee."

Merry smiled wryly. "If only Bourne could tell me whether it was accident, suicide—or murder."

ROSELINE DAJOUSTE NEVER worked weekends, and she had the Monday holiday off as well. But David Murphy managed to track her down that Saturday afternoon while she was examining the produce, freshly picked from the fields wilting under blazing July heat, at Bartlett's Farm. The market would be closed July Fourth, so Roseline was planning ahead. Her grandchildren were coming over from Hyannis.

"We need you at a family conference," David Murphy said when she answered her cell phone. "There are decisions that must be made regarding my father's future, and they can't be made without you."

He was tiresome, Mr. David—she had never liked him so well as Mr. Elliot. He was a cold man and she doubted that her loyalty counted for much. But he paid her salary out of his father's accounts, and the Murphy household was Roseline's sole source of income. She bagged up her wax beans and lettuce and a few of the very first tomatoes, paid for them hurriedly, and drove back out Hummock Pond Road to town.

She was just getting out of her car when Meredith Folger arrived.

"THAT BAG OF coffee beans?" Elliot said blankly. "I threw it out. Andre bought some fresh beans yesterday afternoon."

"Can you retrieve it from the trash for me, Mr. Murphy?" Merry asked.

"If you really want me to."

He had answered the front door, which was helpful, she thought. She hadn't brought a search warrant; Step Above was technically still a crime scene and everything in the house was possible evidence. But as a lawyer, David Murphy might try to thwart even simple requests. His first instinct would be to shield his father. Elliot was less cautious.

She and Roseline DaJouste followed him into the kitchen, where he rummaged through a trash bucket under the sink. She didn't bother to give him plastic gloves like the ones she was wearing; his prints were already all over the evidence.

"Here." He handed her the half-empty bag of Chester's Blend. "Nice I didn't toss this in the garbage can in the garage. It'd stink to high heaven in this heat."

Merry glanced inside the crumpled sack. Still a mix of light seeds and brown beans.

Roseline was moving between them, settling her bags of produce in the refrigerator. "I'm just leaving those here, Mr. Elliot, until I go home. You don't mind, do you?"

"Of course not. I'm sorry you had to come over today."

Merry sealed the mix of coffee and apricot seeds in an evidence bag. "Mr. Murphy, I'm going to lock this in my car. Then I'm coming back inside. I'd like to speak to your brother and his daughter, if I may."

"Just them?" asked Elliot. "Not all of us? Laney's mother arrived a half-hour ago."

"For now, just them. Next, I'd like to interview Roseline."

The housekeeper darted a glance at Elliot. "I am expecting houseguests off the five o'clock ferry. How long will this take?"

"Only a few minutes, I promise you," Merry said.

⟡

DAVID AND LANEY joined Merry in Spencer Murphy's den. David had seated himself behind his father's desk; Laney sat alone on the sofa. Merry shut the door on the rest of the household and set out her laptop on the coffee table. She was without Seitz as note-taker all day; he was busy on the checkpoints leading into Nobadeer.

"I assume you have something to tell us about my sister's death," David said. "Although why you couldn't inform the entire family—"

"Your sister was poisoned," Merry said briskly. "An organic cyanide compound was found in the residue of her coffee mug. Presumably she drank it."

"So she killed herself?"

"Like Alan Turing," Laney murmured.

"I'm sorry?"

She looked at Merry. "Alan Turing. An English code-breaker during World War Two. He was gay and that was against the law, then, so he put cyanide in an apple and ate it. It was a movie with Benedict Cumberbatch."

"Laney," her father said impatiently.

"I remember." Merry looked back at her keyboard. "I don't know whether your sister committed suicide, Mr. Murphy. I only know, for the moment, that there was cyanide in her coffee. She may have ingested it by mistake, on purpose—or someone may have wanted to kill her."

David laughed skeptically. "There was nobody here to kill her."

Merry glanced up, her fingers stilled. "Your father was here. So was Roseline DaJouste. I have to take seriously the possibility that one of them put the poison in her coffee."

"That's absurd," he said flatly.

"Possibly. But I assume as a lawyer you've been trained to weigh evidence. You must see that it can't be ruled out."

"Where would either of them get poison? Never mind *why* either would want to kill Nora," he countered.

"Organic cyanide is found in dried apricot seeds. It's a chemical called laetrile."

Laney drew a quick breath. "I wasn't here when Nora died," she said. "I didn't even know I had an aunt."

Interesting, Merry thought, as she typed that phrase into her notes. "Ms. DaJouste has said that you, Mr. Murphy, have also not been in the house since Christmas. But of course, she leaves work around 5:30 P.M., and can't vouch for any visits you might have made to Nantucket at night."

"I last left Nantucket for Boston on Cape Air December twenty-eighth," he said. "The first time I've returned is today. I'm sure as a police officer you can access the airline's records. Are you planning to have us sign printed statements, Detective? Because if so, I'm not sure Laney and I should talk to you without criminal counsel."

"Dad—"

"That's your choice." Merry met his rigid gaze. "I'm trying to establish some simple facts so I can figure out how and why your sister died in this house. We found apricot seeds in a bag of coffee she may have used in the self-grinding coffeemaker you brought at Christmas. I'm told your father never turned it on. But it's possible you, or your daughter—who brought the apricot seeds to this house a year and a half ago, as a natural cancer treatment—mixed up the seeds and the coffee beans. It would help me to hear a simple yes or no from each of you."

"I don't drink coffee," Laney whispered.

"And I don't need laetrile," David added. "Maybe Nora liked dried apricot seeds. Laney says they're a popular snack in India and the Middle East. "

"Snacking on the seeds wouldn't kill her," Merry said. "The human body can digest and metabolize a few each day, which is why people risk eating them. Particularly cancer sufferers. But ground up with beans in the coffee-maker and steeped in boiling water, the seeds would have released a toxic dose of cyanide. Did either you, Laney, or you, David Murphy, mix the apricot seeds and coffee beans in the same bag when you were here at Christmas? Yes or no?"

Laney glanced fearfully at her father. "No."

"No," he echoed. "I'm guessing Nora did that herself. Maybe she had a death wish."

"Like Alan Turing," Merry said.

"Exactly," the lawyer replied.

THERE WAS NO point, Merry realized, in taking the coffeemaker as evidence. Elliot and Andre had been using it without ill effects for the past two days. Any cyanide from the apricot seeds would have been confined to the ground contents of the filter basket and any remaining coffee in the pot—but both were probably thrown out the very day Nora Murphy died.

"Do you remember Miss Nora making coffee with this machine, Roseline?" Merry asked as they stood together in the kitchen.

"She always drank Mr. Spence's coffee. He makes it on the stove, in the percolator."

"Okay. Are there any days when he *doesn't* do that?"

"Some mornings he goes down to that club on the docks," she said, "and has coffee with his friends."

"The Wharf Rats."

Roseline nodded.

"Can you remember if he had coffee with the Rats during the week Miss Nora disappeared?"

Roseline tapped her lips with her fingers, her eyes fixed on the scuffed linoleum floor. "Yes," she said. "We were out of canned coffee. He told me one night when I went to say goodbye, and asked me to pick some up in the morning on my way back here. He would go to the club, he said, before I arrived. He was sitting with Miss Nora out back, smoking his cigarettes, which he had not done in a long time."

"What time do you arrive in the mornings?"

"Around ten o'clock."

"And that morning—when you brought the new can of coffee—what do you remember?"

"Mr. Spence was out," she said slowly. "At his club, like he said."

"And Miss Nora?"

"Nowhere to be seen."

"And this new coffee machine?"

Roseline lifted her eyes to Merry's face. "Plugged in. Warm. With coffee in it. I remember now—I put the pot and basket in the dishwasher that night. I had made dinner for both of them, but Miss Nora never came back for dinner. It was the day she disappeared."

ON HER WAY back to the station, Merry stopped at the offices of Cape Air, which were housed in the small gray-shingled building that served as Nantucket's Ackerman Field airport terminal.

"Cindy," she said to a harassed woman who was managing people bumped from overbooked holiday flights out of Hyannis, New Bedford, Boston, and White Plains, "I need to know whether a guy named David Murphy ever flew in from Logan between January first of this year and May thirty-first."

Cindy pulled a pen out of her elaborate French knot of brown hair and scribbled down the words. "Got a warrant to search our database?"

"Not on Saturday."

"Okay, then." Cindy smiled widely. "I'll let you know in an unofficial capacity by tomorrow. If you need it official, come back Tuesday with the right piece of paper."

Chapter Nine

DAVID PUT HIS arm around his father's shoulders as the two of them walked slowly down the hall to his bedroom after dinner. Andre had cooked for all of them that evening—swordfish on the grill, with a marinade he said had come down through his grandmother from Haiti. He'd served a curried rice salad with it and peach salsa he incongruously dressed with champagne vinegar and bacon. They had opened several bottles of crisp white wine—a white Bordeaux and a pinot gris from Oregon. Everyone except David seemed to be enjoying themselves.

Andre, he thought, had completely infiltrated the family. Laney had talked more today than she had in months. Her pale skin was flushed with sun and she smiled easily. Kate sat at Andre's end of the table, occasionally touching his arm as she cracked a joke or made a point. They didn't seem to feel the awkwardness he did around his brother's partner. But then, they hadn't grown up with a guy who'd made them see, at twenty, that they had never really known him at all. By now, David recognized that the casually homophobic comments he'd made all his life had been unwittingly devastating to his relationship with Elliot. He was fairly confident that his brother had shared every one of them with Andre. Who was trained to analyze people. Was it any wonder David could barely look him in the eye?

It was left to David to entertain his father at dinner. When Spence asked him several times how his work was going—and then betrayed that he thought David was a reporter, not a lawyer—he decided he was done. Elliot was serving *his* contribution to the meal—a blueberry crumble—but David pushed back his chair and tossed his napkin on his placemat. "Dad's tired," he said. "I'm going to walk him back to his room."

Now Spence sat on the edge of his bed and looked up at David through filmy eyes. It crossed his mind that his father probably suffered from cataracts on top of everything else, but it could hardly matter. "Do you need help getting into your pajamas?" he asked.

Spence frowned. "Are you kidding me?"

But he had trouble bending over to untie his shoelaces, so David knelt at his feet and did it for him. "We should get you slip-on shoes."

"Slip-ons tend to fall off."

David went to a drawer and pulled it open. "Dad. Do you remember the coffeemaker I gave you at Christmas?"

"I perk all my coffee."

"I know. Do you remember the coffeemaker?"

"No."

"I left some coffee beans in the cupboard. In a bag. It was open, because I used the coffeemaker at Christmas."

"What coffeemaker?"

David handed Spence his pajamas. Spence stared at them, as though uncertain what they were for. "Do you remember the dried apricot seeds Laney gave to Mom, when she was sick?"

"Your mother's sick?"

David closed his eyes. "Do you need any help, Dad?"

"No. But I think I'll take a little rest. I'm awfully tired. That interview today wore me out."

The interview, David realized, had been with Meredith Folger. He doubted she had learned anything more from Spence than he had.

"That's a good idea," he agreed. "Just lie down."

HE WOULD HAVE given anything to leave the rest of them playing board games in the living room, and creep upstairs to read through some documents in bed for the next several hours, but there were decisions to be made. He couldn't stay absent from his office forever. There were too many critical matters pending on his desk. So he forced himself to walk back to the main part of the house, and found it empty except for Andre. The others must be doing the dishes. Andre was sitting with a laptop on his legs, a slight frown between his eyes, scrolling through email.

"Thanks for dinner," David said, and reached for a copy of the *Boston Globe* lying on a table.

"You're welcome. Nothing beats harpooned sword."

"I can't really cook."

Andre flashed his contagious smile. "You should try it, Dave. It's a wonderful way of exploring different cultures without leaving the house."

"I don't really care about food. If I could take a pill in place of each meal, I would."

"Except for coffee, right?"

David accordioned the paper. "What does *that* mean?"

Andre's eyebrows rose. "Your machine. It's fabulous. El

and I have really loved using it this weekend. We're talking about buying one when we get back to New York."

"Be glad it didn't kill you," David said.

Andre frowned, but then his gaze shifted to the room's arched doorway. "Hey, girls. Thanks for dish-duty."

"That's a deal I'll make anytime," Kate said. "But tomorrow Laney and I will handle dinner, okay?"

"I thought you were leaving tomorrow," David said.

She looked at him. "Before the funeral?"

"It can't matter to you. You're not part of this family."

Kate sighed and sank down into an ancient wing chair. "Do we have to have this conversation again, David? Were you waiting until Spence went to bed to order me off the property? He doesn't want me to leave. He said so."

"By this time, Kate, he doesn't even remember you're here."

David glanced around the room. Elliot was sitting next to Andre with his hand on his thigh. Laney was still standing in the doorway, her happiness fled, as though she was thinking of going straight up the stairs.

"Sit down, Laney."

She hesitated an instant, then huddled on the floor at the foot of Kate's chair. David pretended not to notice she was taking sides. He had always known she lived with him solely because her room and board were free.

"We couldn't talk about any of this at the dinner table because of Dad. But we should discuss it now," he said. "Detective Folger informed me this afternoon that Nora was poisoned, probably by the bitter apricot seeds we found mixed into the coffee beans. Those seeds apparently contain cyanide. Laney didn't know that, of course, when she gave them to Nana Barb as a cancer treatment."

"Are you suggesting Laney's responsible?" Kate objected. Her hand went to her daughter's head, smoothing her hair.

"Of course not. Somebody mixed up the two bags— one of seeds and one of coffee beans. It can't have been Nana, because I only brought the coffeemaker and bag of beans here at Christmas, after she passed away. That leaves Laney and me—which is unlikely, as Laney doesn't drink coffee and I never looked at the seeds."

"Or Dad and Roseline," Elliot interjected. "It must have been an accident."

"The police seem to think so."

"Could Nora have done it herself—on purpose?"

"That's what I thought, Uncle El." Laney's voice was practically a whisper.

"Suicide is a possibility," David conceded, "except that Nora didn't leave a note. She made it hard to find her body. And she would have known that Dad might be blamed. I doubt she'd leave him open to police suspicion like that. Me or Elliot, sure, but not Dad. She actually cared about him."

Elliot's brow crinkled. "Suspicion? The police aren't suggesting . . . They don't think that—"

"Roseline or Dad murdered Nora? I doubt they can find a motive." David surveyed their blank faces. "Rose-line seems to have liked her, and we know Dad was crazy about her. But I would expect the idea has crossed the detective's mind."

"Poor Spence," Kate murmured. "He'll be beside himself if he hears it was those seeds that killed Nora. Particularly if he mixed up the bags."

"He'll forget about it," David retorted. "Which is what

we really need to talk about tonight—what are we going to do about him?"

There was a silence. Laney studied her fingers.

"He obviously can't live here alone any longer," David persisted. "He's too confused. He's a danger to himself and other people."

"We could find a care facility," Kate suggested.

"Not on the island." David's voice was like a slap. "I've checked. There are no available beds."

"Boston, then."

"Care facilities are incredibly expensive." He went on as though Kate hadn't spoken. "As Dad's executor, I have no desire to drain his estate paying for twenty-four/seven memory care."

"Dave," Elliot protested. "Dad can afford it."

"He could live for years. Run out of funds. We should put off that transition as long as possible."

"What about hiring a nurse?" Elliot suggested.

"On top of Roseline's salary? It'd be as much as the care facility."

"Roseline already works long hours," Andre said. "And she's a housekeeper, not a caregiver."

"I wanted her here when we discussed the future. But her grandkids were arriving and there was no opportune time with Dad underfoot. I think Roseline will be open to whatever we ask. It's in her interest to keep her job."

"But she's getting older, too," Andre said quietly. "Spence is a big guy, and if he starts wandering, he could be difficult to restrain. Two people are probably necessary. And one of them ought to be a nurse."

"Even a nurse won't solve your problem at night," Kate added. "You're going to have to hire multiple people, David. Instead of this patchwork of care, I'd go with a licensed facility, or even a group house on the mainland—"

"Dad won't want to leave Nantucket," David said. "This is his home. His friends are here, down at the Wharf Rats. Mom is buried here. I'm asking you to think about this creatively."

Elliot held up his hands in supplication. "By all means. I've never heard you ask such a thing before."

David ignored the barb. "Laney's underemployed these days. She doesn't like living with me. There's plenty of room here, on the other hand. She could move in and be responsible for Dad at night."

His daughter stared at him. "Are you serious?"

"You always say you love this place."

"I do, but—"

"And you claim to love your grandfather."

"Of course. But—"

"You could help us all out by actually earning your keep. Which you're not doing now."

"David," Kate said warningly.

Laney looked wildly between them. "He has to be kidding! Grandpa killed somebody, and he wants me to *live* with him? Are you crazy?"

"It won't happen again," David insisted. "He's more likely to kill himself than anyone else. But you and Roseline between you can keep him safe."

"Mom," Laney said, "make him stop!"

"You could at least think about it." David felt increasingly angry. "Give a little *back*, instead of constantly take, take, take."

"*David*," Kate said more firmly. "We'll talk about this

later, Lane. You're not going to be forced to do anything
you don't like."

"Maybe if she had been, once in a while," David
retorted, "she wouldn't lie around the house like a failed
princess!"

Kate rose from her chair. "We're going up to bed,
David. When you can listen to reason about Spence, tell
me. I'm a nurse, remember."

"You haven't worked in years."

She stalked out of the room.

Laney followed her.

David thrust back his seat and went after them.

But he didn't get far.

His ex-wife and daughter were standing stock-still in
the hallway.

Spence was seated in one of the Windsor chairs that
flanked the drop-leaf table. He still hadn't put on his
pajamas.

His father's head was in his hands. It was clear he'd
overheard everything David said.

"DO YOU THINK it's murder?"

Merry set aside her dinner plate and stroked Ney's
head. The dog was sitting alertly between her and Peter,
nose twitching at the odor of pulled pork that rose from
their plates. She had brought home takeout from the barbecue place down on Straight Wharf, whose food they'd
discovered during the off-season. The bar was inviting,
the playlist was blues, and on weekends they offered live
bands. Summer crowds made getting a table impossible,
but her seat on Peter's back deck was idyllic enough.
With the added advantage that they could talk in peace.

"In any other circumstances, absolutely," Merry replied. "Cyanide latte doesn't come along every day." She found a stray French fry and slipped it to Ney. "But it doesn't add up, Peter. The woman's father doted on her. The housekeeper barely knew her. What possible reason could either of them have to kill her?"

"Maybe the housekeeper was afraid Nora wanted to move in and take her job. Does Roseline have any other source of income?"

"No," Merry said. "But she's employed by David Murphy, who handles her salary—I checked. He's the only one in the family who can fire her. All Roseline had to do was inform him that Nora was in the house, and he'd probably have flown over immediately from Boston to kick his sister out. There was no love lost between them."

"Really." Peter rose with the plates. "So mine isn't the only dysfunctional family in the world?"

"Not in the slightest. Is there any more red wine?"

"An entire cellarful."

"You pick."

He brought back a fresh bottle of zinfandel and proceeded to uncork it. "How are you going to crack the victim's secrets?"

Nora Murphy's laptop was resting on the far side of the table, awaiting Merry's attention. But for Bob Pocock and his ultimatum—charges and a case on his desk in thirty-six hours—she'd be relaxing tonight.

"Already done. Phil Potts turns out to be a computer geek. He hacked her security controls."

Peter's brows rose. "Unplumbed depths."

"That phrase always makes me think of sewers."

"Mind if I sit here with you?"

"Not at all," she said gratefully.

He passed her a glass of wine, flipped open his tablet, and began to read.

Merry took a sip of zinfandel, turned on Nora Murphy's laptop, and scanned the icons on the screen. Email, various documents, an accounting program—probably for tracking expenses. A search engine icon. Facebook. And a document titled *Truth*.

She should check the email for Nora's contacts—some of them might prove useful—but first, she clicked curiously on *Truth*.

The opening page was headed Chapter One.

I was born in the season of the monsoon, in the time of fitful sun, when the known world is drowned and nothing is as it seems.

HALF AN HOUR later, the summer heat had dropped.

"It's getting chilly," Peter said. "Want to move inside?"

Utterly absorbed, Merry didn't respond.

He kissed her platinum hair gently.

"Peter," she said. "Nora's book? It's about Spencer Murphy and his time in Laos. And from the first few chapters—it looks pretty explosive."

Chapter Ten

My parents met in the valley of Long Tieng. It is a special place, rising more than three thousand feet above sea level, and ringed by mountains on three sides—challenging terrain for planes and runways. And yet, by the late 1960s, this area the Lao call "the Most Secret Place on Earth" was one of the busiest airports in the world. A valley so empty it was unmarked on maps was home to nearly forty thousand people. There were Hmong tribesmen and South Vietnamese soldiers and Thai mercenaries. There were American Special Forces and men who worked for something called the Special Activities Division, which is part of the CIA, and pilots who flew the agency's planes for Air America. There were women who set up shop in the mud streets of the sprawling encampment that lined the runway, cooking noodles and tailoring clothes and taking in laundry and sometimes the men themselves. The unofficial mayor of Long Tieng was a CIA officer named Jerry Daniels, who had founded the pop-up town as a base camp for the Americans' chosen Lao ally, Major General Vang Po, of the Royal Lao Army. Long Tieng existed so that US forces could penetrate the Ho Chi Minh Trail that ran along the North Vietnamese border with Laos. It had no other reason for being. When the CIA left, everyone else would leave, too.

My mother, Paj, was the wife of Thaiv Haam, who had been educated in Vientiane and spoke fluent French. He also spoke some English. He worked as a translator for the Americans, but later traveled to Vientiane, where there were reporters, he knew, who wanted information about the Most Secret Place on Earth. That was where he met Spencer Murphy, a grinning journalism veteran of the chaos in Southeast Asia who was tracking the dominoes—South Vietnam, Cambodia, Laos—as they fell to Communist insurgencies one by one. Murphy bought Haam a Harvey Wallbanger at a Western-only bar. Haam agreed to show him Long Tieng and hire on as his interpreter. It seemed a simple bargain. A deal between allies.

Thaiv, in Hmong, means "to shield." My mother's name, Paj, means "Flower."

My name is Nora. From the Latin Honora—*or honor.*

There is Destiny in all the ways others choose to name us.

"IT FEELS LIKE revenge to me," Elliot said.

He and David were sitting under an umbrella at a table near the tennis courts at the Nantucket Yacht Club. It was a private club founded over a hundred years before. Their father had been a member in good standing for nearly four decades, skippering a classic 1930s wood-hulled boat designed by John Alden. He'd discovered it one summer at an islander's yard sale and meticulously restored it. Over the years, he'd competed in the Opera House Cup each August with a hand-picked crew of cronies. His sons had learned to sail in a Beetle Cat, which was known as a Rainbow on Nantucket, because each catboat had a different solid-colored sail. The Yacht Club had come up with the idea so that parents could recognize their kids' boats from a distance during weekend races. The Rainbow Fleet, as it came to be called, had been a familiar sight around the island since 1926. The boats were as iconic as a Wianno Senior off Hyannis Port.

Spence had allowed Nora to sail the family Rainbow during her Nantucket summers until she was eighteen. When she had disappeared for college and the world, he sold the catboat and concentrated on skippering his Alden. Those were the epic Opera House Cup years, nearly a decade of competition. He'd had a decade of gentle cruising after that. But as his eightieth birthday approached, Spence had capitulated and sold his beloved boat. That was the year Barbara was first diagnosed with cancer. He'd had other priorities than sanding hulls and varnishing teak. His Yacht Club membership remained.

David and Elliot's sailing days were long behind them. This morning they had walked down from Lincoln Circle to trade sets of tennis. They had greeted old friends of their father's and people they'd known themselves as adolescents, both of them secretly astonished at how badly everyone had aged. Now they were drinking iced tea and lemonade with a view of the harbor. The Yacht Club was swathed in red, white, and blue, but it was an oasis of sanity on July 3rd, as crowds of weekenders and day-ferry tourists milled up Main Street, over Centre, and down Broad.

"My plan to keep Dad on the island. How is that revenge?" David asked. "He loves it here."

"Revenge against *Kate*. By making poor Laney miserable."

"Laney's never been poor in her life." He stared steadily at the blue water of the harbor. "I'd just like to see whether she can accept a challenge for once. Do something necessary, whether she likes it or not."

"I talked it over with Andre last night. He agrees that we should move Dad to New York," Elliot said. "Assisted living. A place that offers graduated levels of memory care. So that if he gets worse as time passes, there are supports already in place. He won't have to be moved again."

"How generous of Andre. Is he going to pay for it, too?" David asked.

"Well—" Elliot hesitated. "Actually, Dave, I might as well tell you. Andre and I are getting married. We were going to announce it this weekend but the whole Nora mess has made it . . . inappropriate somehow."

"Don't," David said.

"Don't what?"

"Get married. You'll end up hating him."

Elliot frowned slightly. "I think we ought to compare costs, between hiring more people on an hourly basis here and paying for memory care in New York."

"But you're not Dad's power of attorney," David said flatly. "I am."

"Maybe we should discuss that, too." Elliot's voice was strained. "I'm not sure it's healthy for any of us to put the Dad-problem solely in one set of hands."

"What does *that* mean?"

"Andre thinks that decisions about Dad's future— whether he stays here or goes, what happens to the house once he's gone—should be equally shared. After all, Dad's leaving Step Above to both of us. You're a lawyer and I'm sure you're a great executor, but your decisions affect my inheritance. The house needs upkeep. We should set aside funds for that, and draw up a schedule of necessary maintenance, now that Dad is no longer capable of managing it. That should happen whether he's living here or not. With all these costs and payments, Andre thinks the process should be more codified and transparent. It shouldn't be something you have to handle alone. I agree."

"You do realize I don't give a rat's ass what Andre thinks?" David said. "He has no more right than Kate to know about any of this."

"But I do," Elliot persisted. "I'd like to go over Dad's assets with you. You know how much of his royalty income is left. I can give you a rough estimate of the house's worth. It's the only way we can make informed decisions about his future."

"It doesn't matter whether the house is repaired or falls down," David said impatiently. "It's the location that will matter to buyers once Dad's gone. Steps Beach is Nantucket's Gold Coast. The house will be razed."

Elliot was shocked. "We're not selling Step Above!"

David tore his gaze from the water and stared at his brother. "Of course we are."

"Since when?"

"Why would we do anything else? The place is a gold mine. We can't keep it. The taxes alone are insane."

"But it's important to us!"

David shrugged. "Not to me. I can't unload it fast enough."

"I love that house! More than anything else in the world!"

"Don't tell Andre that." He pushed back his chair and rose from the table, jiggling the remaining ice in his drink glass. "When Dad dies, you can buy me out. But I reserve the right to an independent appraisal. Forgive me if I don't take yours as gospel."

"David—" Elliot was despairing. "You *know* it needs a ton of work. A new foundation, probably. New wiring and windows. A new *roof*. New plumbing and a new septic field. Which means new landscaping. And that doesn't even *begin* to touch the actual renovation. Of the interior space, I mean."

"Oh, God. Don't tell me. You have blueprints drawn up in your head."

"The house deserves to be brought into the twenty-first century. That's going to cost significant money."

"Which is why we should sell it."

"You might feel differently if you saw the place as it *could* be," Elliot argued. "Not a falling-down wreck with an unmown lawn, but a jewel of a place to entertain your clients. I'm amazed you haven't thought of that before, Dave. It's such a quick flight from Boston. We'd be willing to let you use it any time you wanted."

David placed his empty glass deliberately on a nearby tray. "My taste is nothing like Andre's. And neither is my clients'."

Elliot flushed. "What's that supposed to mean?"

"It means Nantucket isn't exactly Fire Island."

"Did you *really* just say that?"

"Yes, Elliot, I did."

"You don't give a fuck about any of us, do you?"

David picked up his racquet and tossed a towel over his shoulder. "I have work to do. I'll see you back at the house."

BECAUSE PETER MASON lived on a farm, he was in the habit of rising early. His foreman, Rafe da Silva, was generally responsible for the flock of sheep that roamed over Peter's acreage—what little of it wasn't bog devoted to cranberries. But since his marriage to Tess, Rafe no longer lived in the apartment above the barn. He drove the six miles from town each morning in semi-darkness to the unmarked sandy track through the moors that led to Mason Farms. By the time his headlights raked across the entrance gate, Peter had already checked the henhouse for eggs and was waiting for him with a fresh mug of coffee. Neither of them talked much in the morning. They stood a few feet apart, hands thrust in their pockets, with the dog, Ney, at their feet. Smelling the air. Feeling the weather. Drinking the coffee as it cooled.

Merry was rarely awake for this ritual. Unlike Peter, she could never get enough sleep. So he was surprised when he reentered the house to find her out of bed and on a stepladder in his library, searching the bookshelves.

"Are you okay?" he asked.

"I'm fine. Do you have anything here on Long Tieng?"

"Long what?"

"Tieng. It's a place in Laos."

"Of course it is," he said resignedly. "Because, Nora Murphy. There should be a book somewhere in the left-hand section—try the upper shelves, not too near the ceiling. *A Great Place to Have a War*. Guy named Kurlantzick wrote it. The spine is orange."

He went back to the kitchen. She would want her morning drink exactly the way she liked it—half steamed milk, half black coffee, in that order. People who didn't know Merry took one look at her straight blonde hair and efficient work clothes and assumed she was low-maintenance. He knew better.

"You're a military historian," she said when he reappeared near his bookshelves.

"In college," he temporized.

She took the mug and handed him *A Great Place to Have a War*. "I don't have time to read this. But I don't know enough about the US involvement in Laos to understand Nora Murphy's notes. Could you summarize for me?"

"Sure." He glanced at her uncertainly. "How much do you know about the Vietnam War?"

"I don't care about that," she said. "I'm asking about Laos."

"But they're connected."

"Okay. Then just—assume I know enough. We were fighting the Communist North Vietnamese, who were backed by the Chinese and the Russians; our allies were the South Vietnamese, who were supposed to be democratic. Fifty thousand US soldiers died and the North Vietnamese won."

"Good," Peter said encouragingly.

"But Laos. From Nora's laptop, she seems to be talking about stuff that happened *after* we pulled out of Vietnam."

"Only kind of." Peter sat down on the sofa. Merry curled up next to him with her nose in her coffee mug. "We weren't supposed to set foot in Laos. Neither were the North Vietnamese. It was a neutral country. But neither side respected that, which is why the warfare there was secret. If you look at a map, Laos is sandwiched between Thailand—a major US staging ground—and Vietnam. The Ho Chi Minh Trail, the principal north-south supply route during the war, ran along the Lao-Vietnamese border. During the rainy season it was impassable for six months and not much happened. During the dry season—which began roughly in December each year—the trail became a North Vietnamese highway to the south."

"Okay," Merry said. "I get it. The CIA set up a base camp in this place called Long Tieng to ambush the North Vietnamese when they were using the trail. And at its height, there were tens of thousands of people in this makeshift city—some American, some Lao or Hmong, as Nora calls them—"

"The Hmong are a hill tribe native to that part of Laos," Peter explained. "They worked for the Americans. And yes, at that point Long Tieng was the second-largest city in Laos, after Vientiane. And yet it was never marked on a map."

"Go on. I shouldn't have interrupted."

"The US involvement in Vietnam ended with the signing of the Paris Peace Accords early in 1973—I think as early as January that year. So American forces pulled out of Southeast Asia in the months that followed."

Merry's eyebrows crinkled. "But Nora's writing about two years after that. At least."

"That's because the Communist insurgency in Laos—backed by their friends in North Vietnam and *their* friends in China and Russia—continued to fight a civil war for control of the country. Same thing happened in Cambodia. In Laos the insurgency called themselves the Pathet Lao. By the spring of 1975 they'd seized control of the government and the capitol, Vientiane. And there were still fifty thousand people—most of them Hmong tribesmen or mercenaries of various nationalities who'd worked for the US—living in Long Tieng. The Pathet Lao made it pretty clear they'd annihilate them as soon as they took the valley."

"So what happened?"

"Oh, it was a disaster," Peter said. "At that point, the only Americans left in Laos were a few diplomats still attached to the embassy and one CIA guy in Long Tieng. He became famous. I've forgotten his name but it's somewhere in this book."

"Jerry Daniels," Merry said. "Nora mentions him."

"Right. Daniels. Anyway—he had one Air America plane and one pilot on the airstrip. And fifty thousand people who wanted out. He got a few more planes sent in from Thailand and managed to evacuate a thousand other people out of the city before the Pathet Lao arrived. The rest were left hanging."

"They always are," Merry said. "So who made the cut? Who got on the plane?"

"Top Lao commanders, people close to the Agency."

"But probably not Nora's parents," Merry suggested. "Her mother was a cook in Long Tieng. She was married to Spence Murphy's interpreter—who, if you remember, was killed."

"I do," Peter said. "I've got a copy of Spence's book right there on the shelf."

"You've read it?"

"You haven't?"

Merry shook her head.

"He witnessed the evacuation of Long Tieng. But he wasn't supposed to be there. He was the only Western reporter on the ground. He refused to leave his interpreter—the guy married to Nora's mother, apparently—and when all three of them were left behind, with the Pathet Lao coming, they did what most of those abandoned in Long Tieng did: they started to walk."

"To where?"

"In Spence's case, south toward Vientiane. The Pathet Lao were there, sure, but so was the US embassy."

"How far away was it?"

"About a hundred and fifty miles, I think. I don't remember exactly."

"Down from this high mountain valley. That was so secret there were no roads."

"According to Spence's book, it took the three of them several weeks to walk out. Nowhere was really safe. There were insurgents in the jungle."

"With knives," Merry mused. "He mentioned that, recently."

"Spencer Murphy wouldn't have survived without his Hmong interpreter—who also saw Spence as his own best chance out of the country." Peter took her coffee mug from her hand and rose to refill it. "It made sense, I suppose. They could wait in Long Tieng for an evacuation that never happened, or make it to the American embassy and get three seats on a plane back to the US. Only it didn't end that way."

"It never does."

"By the time Spence reached the capitol weeks later, the US embassy was shut down. Everybody had gone home. Being the only American on the ground in that situation must have been terrifying."

"Maybe," Merry said. "But being the only American on the ground made it possible for him to lie."

Chapter Eleven

MERRY DROVE STRAIGHT from Mason Farms that Sunday morning to Steamboat Wharf, at the end of Broad Street, where the 8:45 car ferry from Hyannis was due. It was Fireworks Day, July 3rd, with a full thirty-six hours to go before the holiday was officially over. Police reinforcements were arriving from all over America, as Nantucketers called the mainland, rolling off the car ferry in marked SUVs. They would be deployed to control the weekend traffic and chaos along with the Nantucket Police, the Community Service Officers, and members of the Nantucket Sheriff's Department.

Merry stood on the tarmac as the cars exited the lot onto Broad Street, and checked off the reserves on her clipboard. Her orders were to dispatch them to the access roads leading to Nobadeer Beach, where the party that had started the day before was still going strong. But she also decided to send a contingent out to Eel Point, between Dionis and Madaket, in case the clever band of revelers spontaneously retreated to alternative ground. It was the sort of intuitive adjustment an islander would predict. Bob Pocock lacked sufficient Nantucket history to anticipate his enemies.

She was staring after the last of the SUVs when the chief walked up to her.

"Sir."

"Made any progress on your cyanide poisoning, Detective?"

Pocock had said he didn't want to hear about the case until July Fourth weekend was over, but clearly he expected an update. Anything to keep her off balance.

"Yes," Merry said. "You'll have my report on Tuesday morning. As you requested."

"I'd rather have it now."

He turned away, expecting her to follow him. With a sigh, Merry handed her clipboard and radio to Howie and trailed after the chief. He led her to the pilings that fronted the parking lot and turned to face her, his thumbs in his belt loops. The sun on his skin exposed a map of faint lines that would be visibly white if he ever tanned. But it occurred to Merry that she'd never seen Pocock outdoors before. He was whiter than she was in the middle of July.

Merry waited for him to break the silence.

"Well?"

"Phil Potts circumvented the security controls on the victim's laptop. She was a journalist who'd been researching an investigative piece in Laos. Turns out that the book outline on Nora Murphy's computer is for a tell-all biography of her father, Spencer Murphy. She planned to expose his first bestseller—*In the Cage of the Pathet Lao*—as a complete fabrication. Bullshit. Lies."

Pocock frowned. "Wasn't that book made into a movie?"

"Yes. It's the basis of Spencer Murphy's public fame and success. It's why he's a national hero."

"So he shut her up," Pocock said, "with poisoned coffee."

"I'm not so sure."

The chief exhaled in frustration. "Yeah, well—you're not convinced this is even a murder case. Still think the woman died on her father's roof by accident?"

"It's a possibility I have to consider."

"This is an open-and-shut case, Detective," he said. "You've got a victim. You've got a man with the means, opportunity, and motive to kill her. And you're not moving on charges?"

"Spencer Murphy suffers from dementia."

"Let his lawyer deal with that when he defends him in criminal court."

"His lawyer's not my concern, Chief." Merry leaned forward to meet him eye-to-eye. "My concern is that a man who can't even remember his daughter was in the house—who has to be reminded repeatedly that she's dead—is unlikely to have retained the details of her research and plan to expose him. *If* Nora Murphy even shared those details with him. We don't know whether she did. But I doubt Spencer Murphy is capable of executing a complex and subtle plan to kill her."

"There's nothing subtle about cyanide."

"But its delivery can be." Merry tried to rein in her irritation. "The cyanide was organic, a nitrile known as amygdalin. It derives from dried apricot seeds, which Murphy's wife used as a natural cancer treatment and left in the pantry after her death. The seeds were accidentally or deliberately mixed with the coffee beans that produced the victim's fatal drink. To murder her deliberately, the killer would have to have mastered a multi-step automatic coffee machine that ground its own beans. Most of us are capable of that; but I'm not convinced Spencer Murphy is."

"So he's snowed you, too," Pocock said.

Merry stared at him. "What?"

"You tell me this guy built his whole life on lies. Now he's convinced you he's demented. You don't see a pattern there?"

"The man went missing for ten hours Friday. He forgot he had a car parked in town. He was raving about the Pathet Lao when he was found."

"—but you said the Pathet Lao story is crap."

Merry was silent.

Pocock studied the line of cars idling before the open maw of the MV Eagle's hold. "Maybe Murphy's as good an actor as he is a storyteller, Merry. Maybe this 'dementia' is a lie like everything else."

Merry frowned. Pocock had never used her first name before.

"So what should I do? Have him cognitively evaluated?"

"That'll happen anyway when he's charged."

"I have no proof of Murphy's guilt," Merry said. "I never will. Aside from a confession—which any counsel worth his salt would dismantle in court."

"Try some shock tactics, Detective. Confront the bastard with the truth, and see how he responds."

"Really?"

The chief stared at her mockingly. "Really. Do you *always* wear kid gloves when you investigate a murder?"

KATE MURPHY FINGERED a blueberry- and teal-
colored angora throw at Nantucket Looms's new location
on Main Street. Laney was examining some pillows a few
feet away. They had slipped out half an hour ago while
Elliot and David were playing tennis, to catch a glimpse
of what Laney called the Real Nantucket. They'd had
coffee and pastry at The Bean on India Street—although
Laney had insisted on her usual green tea—then strolled
around the shops with the rest of the lighthearted summer
crowd. Kate had forgotten how much she loved the old
brick and cobblestoned town. How special it was, with its
utter lack of national chains, neon lights, or even traffic
signals. She would give anything to return when David
wasn't in residence at Step Above—rent a bike and go all
over the island off-season, to revisit places and moods she
had once loved. Perhaps if Laney *did* stay with Spence—

But her heart sank suddenly at the thought. Spence a
year ago would have been a lot of fun, with his unquench-
able talent for storytelling and his boisterous love of life.
Spence today . . . Spence today had asked her repeatedly whether she was still nursing in Boston. Kate had
answered with infinite patience. By the fourth iteration,
she simplified her reply. *Not anymore*, she offered, instead
of the tangled reminders of all he'd once known about
her divorce, upheaval, settlements, relocation.

Kate had been so sure that Spence understood everything about her plans for the future. She'd *told* him all
about the organization she had in mind—a place where
her background as a nurse and her administrative talent
would be equally valuable. He'd encouraged her to move
on with her life at Barbara's funeral, where the memory of
roads not taken seemed to occupy his mind. In fact, it was

his implicit promise of financial support that had given Kate the courage to leave David. But Spence's mental decline had accelerated in ways she hadn't expected. It was obvious he had no memory of her plans or his promises. And his emotions were increasingly unpredictable.

His anger last night had been a shock. She saw again in her mind how Spence had risen from the Windsor chair in the front hall and hurled himself at David.

"Are you accusing me," he'd roared, "of *killing Nora?*"

There had been no way around it, then. Spence had charged into the living room and demanded explanations from all of them. They had tried, as best they could, to calm him—Elliot insisting that Nora had simply died and no one knew why—but he was in one of his rare lucid passages, fresh from a brief rest, and he refused to go quietly. David had eventually convinced him to drink a shot of brandy. He told Elliot later he'd dropped a Benadryl in it to help his father sleep.

At breakfast, the storm appeared to have passed. Spence was just as usual; he never mentioned Nora's name. His confusion was obvious. Kate was kind to him but kept up a bright flow of conversation with Andre about his shelter work. He and Elliot were firmly on Team Kate, she knew, and after David's frozen hostility it was a relief to compare New York notes, talk restaurants and jazz clubs and real estate and clients. In front of Spencer, neither of them mentioned the dreadful news Meredith Folger had brought yesterday. But cyanide was all the rest of the family could talk about, in groups of two or three, once the older man was safely shut in his room. They were each convinced that Spence had committed a fatal error.

"Grandpa's so much worse," Laney said now.

She was holding a pair of earrings to the light of the sunny front window, turning them like a spirit-catcher. She had retreated into herself since David's proposition the night before—relieved, Kate thought, that Spencer's outburst had diverted her father's attention. David always made her suffer, Kate thought bitterly. He liked knowing that he could tear his daughter's heart in two. By treating Kate like a hated enemy ever since she'd arrived, he'd handed Laney a choice. Which parent had her loyalty? Which was she willing to lose? He'd never appeal to Laney's love or support. David didn't care how much you gave. He cared what you gave up.

"You were here at Christmas," Kate said. "Was his memory as spotty then?"

Laney shook her head. "The good periods were longer. The bad ones seemed like mistakes. Now it's the reverse."

Kate slid the elegant throw one last time against her cheek, then slipped it regretfully back into a stack of similarly gorgeous weavings displayed on a ladder-back chair. Her budget was far too tight to allow splurges. "It's obvious he can't live alone any longer."

"Of course not! He just killed someone! He could be sent to jail, Mom!"

"Not jail, sweetheart."

"He should be," Laney whispered. "So should I."

Kate realized suddenly that it wasn't just David's anger that had throttled her daughter the previous night at dinner; it was the sick comprehension that an aunt she'd never met had died from apricot seeds Laney brought to the house. David might argue that Nora could have committed suicide. He was a lawyer. He had spent his life negotiating ambiguities. But Laney was absorbed in horror. Her grandfather was losing his mind. And between them, they had killed a woman.

"You have absolutely no reason to blame yourself," Kate said firmly. "You tried to help Nana Barb with the best intentions possible."

"He doesn't even remember," Laney persisted, "that Nora's dead. Much less *why* she died. It's so creepy, Mom. Sometimes I look at him, and he's Grandpa. But sometimes there's nothing in his eyes. He looks at me like I'm a stranger."

"I think he knows our faces. But he's not always able to put names to them."

"Can we just . . . get out of here? Can we just leave right now?" Laney's face was hauntingly white. "I'm really freaked out. I didn't sleep well last night. I can't even eat anymore. I mean, what if he . . . poisons *us*?"

"It's not going to happen, Lane." Kate pulled her daughter close. "You know it's not."

"What if those seeds killed Nana, too? What if it wasn't really the cancer? What if she died because I—"

"*Laney.*" Kate shook her slightly. "No. You're not responsible for that. You're not responsible for Nora, either."

"I never even knew her," Laney said. "But she'd be alive, Mom, if I hadn't left those seeds for Grandpa to find."

MERRY DROVE TO Step Above straight from the Steamboat Wharf parking lot. David Murphy answered the door.

"Yes?" he asked, as though she were a stranger. "Can I help you?"

"I'd like to speak to Mr. Murphy."

"Concerning what, exactly?"

"His daughter," Merry said.

David's flat gray eyes surveyed her coldly. "You've already spoken to him once. There's nothing more he can tell you about Nora's death. He probably doesn't even remember it. He's not in command of his faculties."

What an old-fashioned word, Merry thought—*faculties*. As though there was an entire university busily chatting away inside Spencer Murphy's head. "I came early in the day, sir, in the hope that your father would be more alert after a good night's rest. I'd like to know more about Nora's emotional state in the days before her death. It might help us to determine whether it was accident or suicide," she added delicately.

She suspected David was hoping for suicide. It would absolve the household of responsibility.

"Very well." He stepped back to admit her to the hall. "But as my father's lawyer, I'd like to be present."

Merry lifted her brows. "I'm not charging him with anything."

"Even so. I insist. He's not a well man, and I don't want him upset."

Merry followed him out to the back lawn.

Spencer Murphy was seated in his plastic Adirondack chair with a pair of field glasses lifted to his face.

"Goldfinch," he said. "Cute little thing."

"Dad, Detective Folger would like to talk to you again." The field glasses slowly lowered. "Ralph's here?"

"No, Dad. Detective Folger."

David had clearly never heard of Merry's grandfather. She touched Spence's shoulder lightly with one hand.

"I'm Ralph's granddaughter. We met yesterday morning, sir. Do you have a few minutes?"

"Sure. Like a drink?"

"No, thank you." Merry drew up the second plastic chair and sat down. David stood behind them, his arms crossed and a frown on his face. The day was growing hotter. A cloud of midges hovered above the unmown grass.

"You told me yesterday that your daughter, Nora, was thinking of writing a book," Merry said. "Did she tell you what it would be about?"

"Me," Spence said. "She was writing about me."

"Your career? Your life?"

"All the old stories from Laos."

"But I thought you already did a book about those, sir. A long time ago. *In the Cage of the Pathet Lao*."

"Exactly," Spence said. "My escape. Did you know I was major news on every television set when it happened? I found that out, after I got back."

David moved restlessly. "You wanted to ask about my sister's mood, Detective, before she died."

Merry ignored him. "Nora was going to write about Laos. Did she tell you why?"

Spence shook his head. "I don't remember. I guess she was just interested."

"A lot of people were interested in your survival, weren't they?"

"Of course. It's a great story."

"And you're quite a storyteller. You're a member of the Wharf Rats, after all. I bet you hold them spellbound every time you tell a tale. Some of your stories are even true." Merry glanced up at David. He looked irritated. "Is the Laos story true, sir?"

Spence snorted. "You'd have known if it weren't. Somebody'd have scooped me by now."

"Unless everyone who could scoop you is dead."

"Detective!" David broke in. "That's enough. I'm going to have to ask you to leave."

"Nora knew the truth," Merry persisted. "Didn't she?"

David came around his father's chair and stood over her. "If we were in court, I'd say that you're leading the witness. Now kindly get out of here."

"You're obstructing a police officer in the line of duty," Merry told him.

"He's not competent to tell you anything!"

"Then maybe I should tell the story myself. I found pieces of it on your sister's laptop." Merry glanced back at Spence. He was staring at the cloud of midges. "You adopted Nora during a post-war trip to Laos. Her mother, who was the widow of your former interpreter, Thaiv Haam, had just died in a Vientiane slum. Nora was in an orphanage."

"Terrible place," Spence whispered.

"You seem to have loved her. The two of you are described as close. But Nora had unanswered questions about her past. A few years ago, she went looking for her birth parents in Laos. What she found confused her. The names of the birth parents she eventually tracked down—Thaiv and Paj Haam—were both Hmong. Which didn't make sense. Because Nora was half-white."

David drew a sharp breath. "Dad, you don't have to listen to this. Would you like to go inside?"

Spence lifted his hand and waved David aside.

"Thaiv worked for you," Merry went on. "Paj cooked in Long Tieng. When that secret place was overrun by the Communists, the three of you were left behind. You promised Thaiv you'd get him and Paj to Vientiane. You'd fly them to safety in the US. You walked as far as a safehouse in the city—but there you were trapped. The American embassy was abandoned. The three of you needed food and water. Thaiv was the one who risked his life to get it. He was ambushed by the Pathet Lao, tortured, and killed."

"He was a good man," Spence said. "Paj—"

"Was beautiful?"

"Yes."

"What does this have to do with anything, Detective?" David asked. "It's ancient history. If you think Nora killed herself because she found out something about her father—"

"Thaiv wasn't her father," Merry said. "Spence was. It was assumed you were with Thaiv, Mr. Murphy, when he was ambushed that night in June. It was assumed you were a hostage, or dead. But in fact when Thaiv didn't make it back to the safehouse, you and Paj swam across the Mekong River under cover of darkness and crossed into northeast Thailand. You disappeared off the map."

"Yes," Spence said. "We found help in a tiny village outside of Udon Thani. Paj cooked. I taught English. We got by."

"How long did you stay with her? Six months? According to your memoirs, you were back in the States by Christmas."

Spence shrugged. His eyelids flickered. He was beginning to tire.

Merry looked directly at David. "The whole time he was missing, your mother pressured the State Department and any news organizations that Spence had worked for. She lobbied for high-level exchanges between neutral diplomats in an effort to get information. They tried to negotiate Spence's freedom. There was just one problem: the Pathet Lao insisted they didn't have him."

"I remember," David said slowly.

He was beginning to understand.

"Even hiding out in his remote Thai village, your dad must have heard some news reports about his supposed capture. He must have realized that people were looking for him. The more time passed, the harder it would be to explain what he'd done. He couldn't walk out of the Thai jungle and tell the truth: that he'd taken a long vacation. Deliberately dropped out of his Western life. He either had to spend the rest of his days in hiding with Paj—or he could walk out of the shadows in the most spectacular fashion possible. He could 'escape' from a Communist insurgency he claimed had tortured him in a cage. I imagine he spent a week at least wandering around alone in the jungle, getting dehydrated, scarred, and dirty—then walked into the nearest major town."

"Udon Thani," Spence murmured.

"That's ridiculous," David cried. "My father was a hero, Detective! Nora was endless trouble. Whatever she left on her laptop is fiction—meant purely to disturb Elliot and me. She wanted to destroy our relationship with Dad—make us question everything we cherish— and claim him for herself. She'd been trying to do that all our lives."

"Odd then, that she died without even telling you she was here," Merry said.

Chapter Twelve

"THIS IS MY trial run for the wedding." Tess wove her way through the group assembled on the back terrace of the Cliff Road house with a large ceramic platter in the shape of a scallop shell. She was passing hors d'oeuvres from Greengage: raw Nantucket oysters in shot glasses, with a dollop of vodka-spiked gazpacho and crème fraiche; roasted beet rounds dusted with pistachios, artisanal blue cheese, and the cranberry balsamic Peter marketed out of Mason Farms; and her signature Greengage plum, shallot, and duck flatbreads, roasted in the restaurant's wood-fired oven.

Ralph Waldo's white brows furled speculatively as he helped himself to an oyster shooter and a flatbread. He was drinking something that Peter's friend Sky Jackson called a Madaket Sunset—a shakered mix of citrus, mint leaves, fresh tart cherries, and Mount Gay rum. Merry was drinking cold rosé. It paired beautifully with the beets. Peter had settled for his usual vodka soda. John Folger had a Cisco Brewers bottle and a hunk of cheese in his hand. Mayling Stern was sipping a gin and tonic.

There was a slight breeze as the heat moved off the land and met the air from the water. The sky was gradually deepening from turquoise to ink, and music drifted upward from Jetties Beach, where the townspeople were spread on blankets and towels, all of them waiting for that final hushed instant before the first rocket shot up over the Sound.

Merry had traded her work clothes for a sundress and sandals. Her legs were shockingly pale, however, compared to everyone else; she was clearly doing something wrong with her life. Georgiana's husband, Hale Whitney, had flown in for the holiday weekend. He was grilling butterflied lamb while his kids—the eldest was fourteen, now—played a wild game of croquet on the adjacent lawn, pounding each other's balls into the hedges and *rugosa* at the edge of the cliff. Hale was grilling corn and peaches and scallops, too; in a moment they would pull out the heavy teak chairs ranged under the white-painted pergola and sit down to eat. But first, Merry snagged some prosciutto and burrata from Tess's son, Will, as he swung by her with a tray. Tess had dotted the burrata with a nectarine and rosemary chutney. The explosion of flavors was stunning.

"*This*," she said, halting Will with a sudden grasp of his arm. "My God! We have to have *this* at the wedding."

"Nectarines in September?" He gave her a quizzical half-smile. "Could be tough. But Mom will pull something out with figs and pomegranates instead. That was on her menu last fall."

He had grown up incredibly over the past year, his first at Boston College. His lean frame had bulked out a bit and the molding of his face had morphed into a man's. He was brown from lifeguarding at Surfside, a coveted job he'd flown home to secure during the off-season. Merry realized with a jolt how handsome Will suddenly was. The gawky kid who'd stumbled over a body in a cranberry bog years ago was long gone.

"Heard you were out at Nobadeer yesterday," she said.

"Yeah. It's a real scene, Mer. Party's still going. Had to be in the chair this morning, or I'd have gone back."

Howie had told her that forty-three people were arrested. There would be more today, and still more tomorrow if the party churned straight through to the Fourth. "Don't you guys have anywhere else to be?"

"Nowhere that we'd *rather* be." Obviously proud of Tess's cooking, Will was still watching her eat the burrata. "Beats working a murder. Pete says you've got one this weekend."

She tucked a strip of prosciutto around an olive and popped it into her mouth. The briny splash against the nectarine salsa and the cured meat was swoon-worthy. "Not sure I'd call it that. It's possible the woman died by mistake. She drank cyanide in her coffee. The question is how it got there."

Merry noticed that the lighthearted conversation around her had stopped. John Folger was staring at her, his beer arrested midway to his lips. Any other year, he'd have known about a suspicious death before she did. But now that the two of them no longer worked or lived together, John was often the last person to learn the details of Meredith's life.

"Ever run into Spencer Murphy at the Wharf Rats, Dad?"

He and Ralph Waldo exchanged glances. "Funny you should ask. We took him fishing for blues off Tuckernuck a few days ago. Why?"

"He can still handle a rod?"

"Of course, Meredith," Ralph said testily. "His memory may be going, but the important things in life remain."

Her impulse to laugh was swiftly checked. "What day was this?"

John Folger set down his beer. "Friday."

"The day his daughter's body was found on his roof walk," Merry said. "The day Spencer Murphy went AWOL for about ten hours. He was out at the end of Tuckernuck with *you* two?"

"Whoa." Mayling Stern was choking on her tonic. "This guy's *daughter* was found dead on his roof?"

"You don't mean Nora?" Ralph interjected. "Good Lord. I must go see Spence. He loved her so."

"So you knew about her?"

"*About* her? Of course, Meredith. I knew *Nora*. I was still chief when Spence brought her back as a toddler from Laos."

Merry told them then about the double disappearance at Step Above—first Nora, who never left the house at all; and then Spence, who failed to come home.

"No wonder he didn't look exhausted or dehydrated when he finally turned up," Merry mused. "He'd been relaxing in the cockpit of your boat, Dad, for most of the afternoon."

"Drinking my beer," John said.

"We'd had coffee with him at the clubhouse first," Ralph explained, "and then we ran into him on the way to fishing. He looked a little bewildered, like he was at loose ends. So John invited him to come see the Whaler. After that, well . . . we weren't going to leave him on the dock all by himself."

"Except you did exactly that, whenever you got back

from Tuck," Merry observed. "Did it ever occur to you that Spence didn't know his way home?"

Ralph looked a trifle alarmed. "He said he'd parked near Old North."

"He was several wharves away, on New Whale Street. He never found his car, Ralph. He wandered into American Seasons late that night, hallucinating about the jungle and asking for a light."

Sky Jackson handed Merry a fresh glass of rosé. "What about the cyanide?" he asked.

They were all looking at her now, except George's kids, who were chasing each other with the croquet mallets. Even Hale had pulled down the domed cover of his gas grill and was pouring out a Madaket Sunset for himself, all ears.

Merry sighed. "I don't mean to bring work with me everywhere I go. This is just a sad case of a man with dementia possibly killing his own daughter by accident. Unless he did it on purpose."

"Oh, Meredith, no," George said. She shot a swift glance toward her children. They were entirely uninterested in what the grown-ups were saying.

"But Spence loved that girl," Ralph objected. "And she was devoted to him."

"Except for the past ten years, when she never bothered to come home. There are some interesting background circumstances I'm still evaluating, Ralph."

"Are you going to charge Spence?" he asked.

"I can't say. Yet."

"Merry." Peter's voice was quiet. "We understand this is an ongoing investigation."

He was giving her an out. She slipped her arm gratefully around his waist.

"How often do you run into Spence at the Wharf Rats, Ralph?" she asked.

"Three or four times a week. He's still a great story-teller, you know—even if he forgets his way home."

"And people's names. And faces," John Folger mur-mured.

"So you've noticed a decline?"

"It's been fairly steady since Barbara died last year. But worse, I think, since the winter."

"You don't think he could be . . . faking it?"

Ralph frowned at her. "For Heaven's sake, Meredith, why would he do *that?*"

Merry shrugged. "To get away with murder?"

There was a pause. All of them looked at each other. The breeze suddenly whipped up, cooler now and danc-ing through the hydrangeas. Merry shivered.

"Dinner," Hale announced.

AT STEP ABOVE, Kate and Laney made hamburg-ers that night and grilled them outdoors under Spence's old charcoal dome. They were both sunburned and tired; they had spent the afternoon tidying the flower beds that ringed the backyard's perimeter. Kate was a dedicated and intelligent gardener, although she had no plot to speak of in Brooklyn. She hated to see Barbara's carefully cul-tivated perennials overrun with honeysuckle, thistles, mulleins, and spurge that had invaded the beds from the cliff scrub below. Laney was enlisted as dead-header. Kate had trained her well in the neat, walled garden where she'd played as a child on Beacon Hill, and at the end of four hours Spence's old metal wheelbarrow was piled high with black trash bags full of refuse.

Kate had wrestled with the canes of the climbing roses, tying them to the trellis with green-coated wire she found in the cluttered garage. It was placed neatly among Barbara's gardening tools; she calculated that they had not been disturbed in several years, since the last summer before Barbara's final illness.

Laney finished out the day by dead-wooding the massive hydrangeas. They were the kind that bloomed on old wood, but they had suffered a lot of winter kill. Laney filled another two trash bags with hollow, withered stems.

"We'll feed and compost them tomorrow," Kate suggested. "That should boost their blooms."

Laney carted the wheelbarrow around to the quahog-shell drive and stacked the trash bags on the backseat of Spence's old Volvo. She had dutifully retrieved it from New Whale Street the previous night, and had kept the keys. Nantucket was fighting a battle with invasive weeds, and the Department of Public Works urged homeowners to dispose of their garden refuse in its high-temperature anaerobic digester, which effectively killed both roots and seeds.

"I'll drive this to the landfill after the holiday," Laney said.

"Let your father do it," Kate urged. "Running errands would be good for him."

Laney wheeled the empty barrow around the far side of the house to where her grandmother's venerable compost pile still sat. Barbara had never thrown weeds on her compost heap because a wise gardener does not seed her restorative soil with tomorrow's enemies. Scraps of vegetables, the rinds of melons, coffee grounds, eggshells, brown paper bags from Stop & Shop, the soft platinum

ash left in Step Above's grates from driftwood beach parties and winter fires, grass cuttings, corn husks and corn
silk, apple cores, corncobs, peach pits, autumn leaves,
withered pumpkins, and, yes, the snipped heads of Barbara's tulips and peonies, had all been laid to rest on
the heap; and worms had eaten them. Laney took her
grandmother's shovel and dug down through the layers,
left undisturbed since Barbara's death, to the moist brown
granulated compost. It had the texture and faint scent of
chocolate cake.

She half-filled the wheelbarrow in readiness for the
morning, propped the shovel slantwise across it, and
trundled it back to the far end of the yard, where she
parked it near the rose trellis.

She took a long, hot shower before she joined her
mother at the grill.

"It felt good to work," she said as Kate exited the
kitchen with a platter of tomatoes. "Dad hired landscap-
ers for Charles Street once you left."

"Of course he did," Kate said. "How's Spence doing
this evening?"

"I'm great, thank you very much," her father-in-law
replied. "So are the flower beds. Barbara would be so
pleased, if she could see them."

He was sitting in one of the plastic Adirondack chairs
not far from his French bedroom doors, watching them
cook. He was nursing a gin and tonic that Andre had
decided he could have, his eyelids half-closed against a pale
gray stream of cigarette smoke. He had been quiet all day.
Laney was uncertain what he remembered of the previous
night's anguish. Or where he'd found the cigarettes. Then
it struck her: there'd been a pack left in Nora's bedroom.

"When did you start smoking again, Grandpa?" she asked.

"While your sister was here."

She didn't bother to point out that she had no sister. "Nora?"

"Yes. She knows all my vices and secrets."

"Like the fact you're a Marlboro man." Laney smiled at him uncertainly and reached for the old clamshell ashtray, half-buried in the unkempt grass. "Here. We don't want to start a fire."

"Nora knew the truth." Spence tapped off his glowing ash, rolling the cigarette between his fingers. "Most people only know the lies. I made a fortune off 'em. Telling stories. Once I started, no reason to stop."

Laney studied him, a faint line between her brows.

"Nora won't write the book, now. Thanks to Kate."

"Kate?" Laney said. "You mean . . . Mom? What did Mom do to Nora?"

Spence didn't answer. He was staring toward the arched trellis at the end of the lawn, his expression blank. His drink was nearly gone.

Kate touched her daughter on the arm. "Run in and get that platter of vegetables. I want to put them on the grill when I turn the burgers."

The screened door slammed behind Laney. Kate quietly reached down and dumped what was left of Spence's gin and tonic into the grass. "I think you've had enough, Dad," she said.

THE ROOF WALK of the Cliff Road house was in much better shape than Step Above's, Merry thought. It was bigger, too, and had been swept that afternoon by the Whitney kids, who had also carried folding chairs up to the attic in anticipation of the fireworks. Peter straddled the open hatch between the roof and the floor below, reaching down for the chairs as Rafe handed them up. There were fifteen people, counting the kids, gathered under the night sky. They were facing north, toward Jetties Beach and the harbor where the fireworks barge was moored. Somewhere over Merry's left shoulder the sun was setting.

Peter had his arm around her waist and her head was resting against his shoulder.

"The view is so beautiful from up here," she said. "I can see the whole world unrolled at my feet."

"—Or as much of the world as matters. The walk has always been one of my favorite places. I used to come up here all the time as a kid. I even asked my dad to build one on the Greenwich roof—as a sort of winter clubhouse."

"He didn't, of course."

"He wasn't in the business of granting whims." Peter surveyed the horizon. "The view would be different, wouldn't it, if the wind farm had gone through? We should raise a glass to the defeat of Cape Wind."

Cape Wind was an energy company that had fought for years to launch the first offshore wind farm along the coast of the United States—in the middle of Nantucket Sound. The idea was to erect one hundred and thirty turbines, each half a football-field wide and rising three hundred feet above the water, on Horseshoe Shoal, a shallow sandbar that sat five miles from Cape Cod and sixteen miles from Nantucket. The wind farm was projected to cost more than two and a half billion dollars and cover twenty-four square miles. The electricity generated would provide power to at least one hundred thousand homes.

But influential local residents on the Cape and Islands had banded together to fight the project, as had local fishermen, the Wampanoag Tribe, and various congressional representatives. The fishermen had sued, claiming that the disruption of spawning grounds and juvenile fish caused by the turbines' construction—Horseshoe Shoal was known as a great place to hook bluefish—would set back local fisheries for years. Geologists had argued that grounding so many massive structures on the shoal would cause the tides to form unpredicted gullies and new bars on the Sound's floor, changing the known boating channels. And Cape Wind had alienated voters by negotiating noncompetitive bids that would have raised utility bills in the short term. They had outsourced construction contracts overseas, which hadn't improved their popularity. So now the first offshore wind farm in the United States sat off the coast of Rhode Island—built by a different company, and on a vastly smaller scale. Although the state of Massachusetts had endorsed wind farms in an effort to shift energy consumption away from fossil fuels, it had barred Cape Wind from bidding on future state wind-farm contracts.

"Global warming," Merry said. "If sea levels rise as much as they are projected to do in the next hundred years, our descendants will never live on Nantucket. This beloved place will be a speck in the ocean, and we will be hailing saviors from this roof walk."

"Impermanence is healthy," Peter said.

"From the man whose ancestors, like mine, founded this island three hundred and fifty years ago."

"And who hopes technology will solve the problem. Without entirely destroying romance and natural beauty."

"Oh, I don't know," Merry said. "I kind of liked the idea of huge white sails turning in the middle of the sea. I bet the turbines would have had guide lights at night. The Sound would be lit up like Christmas. People would start partying out there in the summertime, popping champagne corks on decks, under the man-made stars."

"I'll take the real ones," Peter said, and kissed her.

At that moment the first rocket went off from the fireworks barge. Automatically, they all cheered.

The sound floated above the greater roar from Jetties Beach below. The rocket exploded in a glare of white light, and Merry caught the sharp silhouette of Peter's profile, etched on her eyelids for seconds afterward. Then the whistle of the second rocket caught them and the sky flowered in vivid petals of green and rose and blue.

She groped behind her for a chair and sat down. Peter leaned against the roof walk's balustrade next to his brother-in-law, Hale, his eyes fixed on the darkening sky.

"Here," Georgiana said. She was crouching next to Merry's chair as though afraid of blocking the view. In her hand was a pashmina shawl. Naturally, being George, she had made sure the color—which was periwinkle blue—complemented Merry's sundress. "It gets cold up here fast at night."

Merry swirled the shawl around her shoulders and allowed herself to feel free, for an instant, of everything but joy in the spectacle bursting in front of her. She'd watched Nantucket's fireworks every year of her life. As a child she'd been forced to sit well back from the waves with her mother while Billy, her older brother, stood seriously with his police chief father and Ralph, barring the staging area on the beach. By the time she was a teenager the fireworks had been exiled to a floating barge anchored in the harbor, in an excess of caution and concern over terrorist attacks. But she'd never seen them from a position like this before, almost on a level with the sky; the spectacle was magical. As the streamers of fire trailed over their heads, Tess Starbuck clapped and hooted like a little girl. She'd never had this view on the Fourth, either, Merry knew. She and Tess weren't Summer People.

"Would you let me know when Nora Murphy's funeral is scheduled?" George asked in an undertone, close to Merry's ear. "If it's not private, I'd like to go. Or at least send flowers."

The cacophony surrounding them almost drowned the words. "Of course," Merry said. "Why?"

"I knew her." George's gaze was fixed on the glittering horizon, her arms wrapped in a coral pashmina. "She spent every summer here as a kid. So did I."

"What did you think of her?"

George smiled through the darkness. "She was one of the coolest people I knew."

A white chrysanthemum burst over their heads, then another, and a third.

"Meaning what, exactly?" Merry asked.

"Oh—probably that she was different from the girls I went to school with in Connecticut all winter long. She was more worldly. Less sheltered. She knew who she wanted to be, and it wasn't part of the herd. She lived in the city during the school year, you know. Her dad was working for CBS then, I think."

"The city, meaning New York?"

George nodded. "I met up with her there, once. Christmas break. My mom invited her to the Plaza for hot chocolate. That was a mistake—I knew it as soon as she walked in. She'd taken the subway uptown and looked about ten years older than she was. I was wearing a party dress; she was in black leggings and boots. Nora was always more of an East Village than a Greenwich kind of girl."

"But you liked her?"

"I wanted to *be* her."

Merry glanced at Georgiana. She rarely suggested there was anything lacking in herself or her world. But one of the things Merry liked most about her almost-sister-in-law was her frankness. George was as authentic as Peter. Like Merry, both Masons had lost a brother and a parent; like Merry, they valued the relationships that remained to them. The people gathered around her under the flaring stars were bound by mutual affection and respect that, with luck, would endure until they died.

"Did you know the Murphy boys, too?" she asked George.

"They were already out of college by the time I met her. One of them was even married, I think. They were like two different generations."

"That's what the brothers say. They don't seem particularly sad Nora's dead."

"No?" George stared at Merry. "I'm sure her dad is. They were incredibly close."

It was the familiar phrase Merry had been hearing for days: Nora and Spence, Spence and Nora, telling exotic stories on the back lawn until one of them disappeared. "And yet, she's been gone for years. They couldn't even find her when their mother died."

"Nora never got along with Barbara," George said. "She used to say all the time that she wanted to know about her *real* parents, and Barb would never tell her. Maybe she didn't know. Maybe the truth was just lost in the war."

Like Spence, Merry thought.

"I wonder if she ever found them," George said.

THEY WERE ALL standing on the east end of the unkempt lawn, well to the right of the rose arbor and the steps down to the scrub and sand, which were lost in darkness, except for Laney—who was sitting alone beneath the arched trellis, her hands tucked into her sweatshirt sleeves and her shoulders hunched. She seemed uninterested in the fiery spectacle bursting in the distance, and Elliot felt a brief flicker of concern. She was so much quieter now than before the divorce. Kate, on the other hand, was infinitely more serene. She and Andre had pulled the two plastic Adirondack chairs over to this spot where the view of Jetties Beach was best, although it was obvious it was a woeful perch compared to the roof walk, which was still roped off with yellow crime scene tape. The two of them had abandoned the idea of sitting, however, and were craning on tiptoe over the neighbor's hedges.

"We should go get Dad," Elliot said.

Spence had eaten his dinner quietly, his head occasionally nodding into somnolence on his chest, and then had allowed David to walk him back to his room while Andre cleared the plates. He and Elliot had done the dishes. By the time they were stacked in the outdated washer, it was nearly dark. They had all drifted separately onto the lawn, Elliot and Andre carrying a bottle of wine, as darkness settled over the Sound. When the first rocket went up from Jetties, each of them jumped. And Elliot laughed. It was the first time he had felt lighthearted in days.

The tide was in, and waves collapsed relentlessly against the shore below them, a muted roar in his ears. Laney seemed fixated on the dark water. Elliot thought of walking over to her—cajoling her to join them—but he remembered what it was like to feel alienated from parents, from the whole world, in a single discordant moment. He left her alone and stood on tiptoe, waiting for the second flare to follow the first. Just past the lights of the beach club that lay between Step Above and Jetties, he could glimpse the fireworks platform moored out beyond the line of surf. A brilliant red-and-blue star burst over their heads.

"Seriously. We need Spence."

"Dad's fine," David said wearily. "He doesn't give a damn about fireworks."

"But what if *we* ought to see them with *him?*" Elliot countered. "This could be the last year he's in the house. The last year he's even partly in his right mind. We should have him here."

"You want to take a group picture, too, and post it online?" David asked sarcastically.

"Andre," Elliot called. "Would you go see if Dad is up?"

"No," David interjected. "He's asleep. Let him rest in peace."

It was a curious choice of words; Elliot could tell he wasn't the only one who thought so by the way Laney's head suddenly jerked around, by the way Kate turned to stare at David. Without a word, Andre walked quietly toward the house.

Another rocket exploded overhead.

"That's a peony," Elliot said.

"Chrysanthemum," David corrected.

"Peonies have fatter streamers. Chrysanthemums are narrow."

"Well, you're the gay guy. I guess you'd know."

His brother said this with complete indifference. It was neither a joke nor a slur. But it was entirely of a piece with what Elliot saw as David's casual cruelty. He didn't care about Elliot's feelings; he never had, from the time they were toddlers together. He'd never congratulated him on his happiness today, when Elliot had announced his plans to marry. Had David always been joyless? Incapable of empathy? Or just since Kate left?

David's eyes were fixed on the fireworks blooming overhead. A weeping willow, Elliot knew it was called—but he didn't tell David that. Instead, he made room for Laney, who had trudged over from the steps to join them.

"Dad," she said.

David glanced down at her.

"Tonight, while Mom and I were making dinner, Grandpa said that Nora knew all his secrets. Which were actually lies. He said he'd made a fortune off them. What did he mean? Are his books just *bullshit*? Did he make them up?"

"What are you talking about, Laney?" Elliot demanded.

"Grandpa!" She wheeled around, her fists balled in her

sweatshirt. "He said Nora was going to write a book about the truth. But that, thanks to Mom, it wouldn't happen now. What did he mean?"

"I have no idea," David said.

"Don't you see?" Laney demanded. "Don't you get it? Grandpa thinks Mom killed her."

Chapter Thirteen

AT 9 A.M. on July Fourth, the Declaration of Independence and the Bill of Rights were read aloud at the Unitarian Universalist church on Orange Street.

At 9:45, the Cyrus Peirce Middle School music teacher sang the national anthem from the steps of the Pacific National Bank at the top of Main Street. The crowd was invited to sing "America the Beautiful" with her afterward, and many of them did. By that time, thousands of people were strolling through the center of town, which was closed to vehicle traffic, and the Orange Street church was poised to strike ten o'clock.

This was the signal to open the dunk tank stationed at the corner of Union Street and Main. People lined up to toss bean bags at it and drown their neighbors.

The watermelon eating contest was staged on tables lined up around the Nantucket Fountain, at the foot of Main Street. Further up, on opposite sidewalks, were face painting and the pie eating contest. A puppet show was scheduled at ten-thirty on the steps of the Methodist church at Main and Centre Streets, and at eleven o'clock the bike decoration contest, including tricycles and wagons, would be judged at the corner of Federal and Main.

But the culminating quarter-hour of the morning's

festivities, from eleven-forty-five until noon, was the real point of Nantucket's Fourth of July. During those fifteen minutes, an epic water fight roared out between the Nantucket Fire Department's hoses—using an antique hand-pumper and a modern ladder truck—and the Boynton Lane Reserves, wielding a LaFrance firetruck dating from the 1920s. Spectators were invited to bring water pistols of their or own, or, alternatively, umbrellas. The entire street party got soaked.

This was Meredith's favorite summer ritual. She'd been dancing under the hook-and-ladders from the time she could walk. But this July she was fated to miss the show. She was assessing the bike decorations critically with Peter when her cell phone rang.

"Detective Folger?"

"Yes, sir?" she said. There was no mistaking Bob Pocock's voice.

"Get out to Lincoln Ave right now. There's been another one of your *accidents*."

SHE FOUND CLARENCE Strangerfield at the foot of Step Above's stairs, to the left of the boardwalk that led across the fifty feet of heather and scrub that separated the cliff from the beach's barrier dunes. The crime scene chief was kneeling in groundsel, wavy hairgrass, sumac, and bayberry. He had wrapped bungee cords around his pants legs to keep them tightly cinched. Clare was deadly afraid of tick-borne diseases. And the corpse might well be crawling with them.

Nantucket was overrun with white-tailed deer, which offered blood meals to legions of ticks in the 50 percent of the island that was conservation open space, as well as the 50 percent that was roads and well-tended backyards, where deer were dismayingly just as plentiful. Adult ticks laid eggs that hatched into baby ticks that became hosts of destructive bacteria—not from deer, but from the mice they infested in their larval stages. Lyme disease was the most obvious illness, but there were others less well-known, like babeosis, which attacked the spleen and was life-threatening and increasingly virulent on the island. Public service flyers distributed on the ferries and in airplanes during the summer season warned of the tick danger, sending steady streams of vacationers into the emergency room.

Clarence's brother-in-law had been flown to Boston with acute babeosis last year.

Merry stepped off the boardwalk into the scrub and picked her way toward the scene. Clarence was photographing the body, which was sprawled facedown. Summer Hughes was kneeling opposite the crime scene chief, a pair of calipers in her hand, positioned over the base of the skull. They had arrived well before Merry—presumably Bob Pocock had dispatched them before calling her. Beyond the two crouching figures Merry glimpsed Nat Coffin, Clarence's assistant, and Joe Potts—both men wearing protective gloves and booties. They were systematically searching through the underbrush for anything that might be evidence.

"Hey, Merry." Summer's eyes drifted past her to the EMTs who were clattering down the steps with a collapsed gurney and body bag.

Clarence glanced over his shoulder. "You want to see him *in situ?*"

She walked forward and crouched down.

Spencer Murphy had bled from a blow to the base of his skull. His sparse silver hair was singed with crimson just above the C-vertebra of his neck. This was bonily visible and poignantly weak with age under his mottled skin. His shoulders were slumped in defeat and awkwardly positioned where he had fallen in the scrub. His legs were doubled beneath him.

His feet, she noticed, were bare.

"Strange posture," she said.

"A-yeh," Clarence agreed. "He landed on his knees."

"Why no shoes?"

"Maybe he didn't like sand in 'em."

Merry frowned at Clarence.

"The family thinks he tried to walk down to the beach in the dark. He'd talked recently about wanting to be here by the water. Asked his granddaughter to help him. He said he didn't trust the railings on his own. I gahther he's not been too steady of late."

"What does it look like to you, Clare?"

"Must've missed the stairs, Marradith, and stumbled off the cliff in the dark."

"How does a man who's lived here for decades miss his own staircase?" Merry demanded. "There's a trellis arch marking the top landing! It wasn't foggy last night."

"No," Clarence agreed. "But if he tripped on the steps I'd expect him to be lying on 'em. There are four different landings between here and the top, for heaven's sake. But he came to rest in the scrub, all the way at the bottom."

Merry peered at the wound. She didn't have to probe it to know that the skull was fractured.

"Doctor? Could this be caused by impact with a wooden railing?"

Summer pursed her lips. "I'd be more inclined to think it was a rock. A chunk of granite hidden by the scrub."

"Which further argues against him going down the stairs," Merry said. "We'll examine the railings, of course—but have Potts and Coffin search the cliff slope for instruments of death, Clare, would you?"

"A' carse."

"Any thoughts about time of death?"

Summer reached for Murphy's arm and attempted to lift it. "He's cool and stiff. In warm weather like this, rigor will have begun to set in pretty fast—say, within two to three hours of death. This rigor is well-advanced, meaning he's already stiffened throughout his body—so I'd estimate he's been dead at least eight hours, possibly twelve. What time is it now?"

Merry pulled out her phone and glanced at it. "Time for the water fight."

"Eleven forty-five," Clarence explained.

"Okay. So if we take conservative parameters for both onset and duration—meaning three hours for rigor to set in, and at least eight hours' duration, possibly twelve right now—I doubt he died much before nine P.M. last night, or was alive much past one A.M. this morning." Summer rose to her feet.

"In the wee small hours," Merry said thoughtfully. "I guess he was a night-wanderer."

But that was before Elliot Murphy showed her Spence's suicide note.

He intercepted her as, in a superfluity of caution, she was sealing off Spencer Murphy's bedroom for Clarence to examine. The French doors to the deck that

Murphy apparently had left open were still propped ajar so that Nat Coffin could dust the knob and edges for finger-prints when he was done searching the cliff face. Merry was stretching yellow crime scene tape across that part of the deck, blocking access. She had done the same in the interior hallway leading to Spencer Murphy's bedroom door. This was still locked from the inside. She would leave it to Clarence's team to dust the interior room knob there, as well.

"Why are you doing this?" Elliot asked in puzzlement. "He didn't die *here*."

"It could be helpful to examine the last room he was in," Merry said blandly.

"That was probably his den," Elliot replied. "I found this note from Dad there, propped against his typewriter. When we couldn't find him this morning I checked the den first."

He handed Merry a sheet of paper. It had been torn from a ringed notebook—probably like the one she'd found in Spencer Murphy's car, with drawings of birds and notes about sightings. On the top right corner was a sketch of what looked like an osprey. There was usually a nest each summer, Merry thought vaguely, out near Madaket. In the middle of the sheet were a few sentences in the same spidery handwriting she'd seen before. *David says I poisoned Nora. How could I do something like that? I can't go on like this anymore.*

She glanced at Elliot. "Your brother told your father that he poisoned your sister?"

"That sounds like a Spanish grammar drill," Elliot retorted. "*Yes, I did not eat the food of the brown cat.* Dad overheard us talking about the cyanide Saturday night. It was an accident."

"They seem to happen all the time in this house." Merry studied the note again. "I noticed Mr. Murphy wrote things down when he needed to remember them. Appointments, people's names, days of the week. Do you think he wanted to remember that David thought he'd killed Nora?"

"I don't know!" Elliot cried. "What does it matter, now? He's gone."

Merry fluttered the notebook page. "The point is *why* these words were written. As a declaration of intent—*I'm so appalled at what I've done that I'm going to throw myself off the cliff*—or as a jog to memory: *David says I poisoned Nora*. This piece of paper doesn't prove suicide."

"Not explicitly. But he certainly left it here last night and he's dead this morning. I wish so much I'd talked to him before bed—maybe I could have stopped him—"

The skin around Elliot's eyes was inflamed and rubbery. He had been weeping.

"When did you last see him?" Merry asked.

"At dinner. I wanted him to watch the fireworks afterward with us, but he'd already gone to bed. When Andre checked on him around nine-twenty, he was asleep."

"He actually saw him?"

Elliot hesitated. "No. He knocked on his bedroom door. Dad didn't answer and the room was dark, so Andre just came back out to watch the fireworks."

So Spencer Murphy was unaccounted for, really, at nine-twenty. It seemed unlikely he'd hurl himself over the cliff while his entire family was watching fireworks on the back lawn—and the Jetties show hadn't ended, Merry remembered, until roughly nine-forty-five. "When did you go to bed, Mr. Murphy?"

"A few minutes before eleven," Elliot said.

"And when did you start to worry about your father's absence this morning?"

"Laney was up first, around seven-thirty. She went out onto the lawn to look at the ocean. When she turned back, she noticed that the French doors to Dad's bedroom door were open. She checked to see if he was there—and found the room empty. The bedroom door to the house was still locked. He must have simply walked outside in the dark and gone over the cliff."

"Was Laney concerned?"

"She knows Spence has been wandering. She knew he was lost Friday. She woke Kate and asked what to do— Kate woke the rest of the house. It was pretty clear Dad wasn't here. I even checked the roof walk, in case—" He halted. "Then I found this note."

"What did you do?"

"I showed it to Kate."

"Not to your brother?"

"David had gone down to the Wharf Rats. He figured if Dad was out and about, he'd head for friends and coffee."

"On the Fourth of July?"

Elliot grimaced. "Dad wouldn't remember it was a holiday, and he'd be standing in front of the closed clubhouse door with a bewildered expression on his face, while the entire world milled around Main Street."

"Understood. So you showed Kate his note."

"It worried her. She thought we ought to call you right away. She said Laney had been feeling responsible, too. Guilty about Nora's death and leaving the apricot seeds in this house. She seemed more worried about Laney

than Dad. So I went looking for Andre. He'd taken our
dog down to the beach—"

Elliot stopped short.

"Yes?" Merry asked.

"It was Tav, actually, who found Dad first. Just like he
found Nora." Elliot smiled faintly. "With that nose, it's
like he's riding shotgun with the Grim Reaper. I'm starting to feel sorry for the little guy."

"OF COURSE HE committed suicide," David Murphy said impatiently. He had sought Merry out as she
barred the doorway to Spencer Murphy's den, this
time, with yellow evidence tape. She wanted the rest
of the desk undisturbed until Clarence's team could
examine the suicide note. "You destroyed his whole
world with your accusations yesterday, Detective.
My father's integrity—his journalistic reputation—
meant everything to him. The things you said were
appalling."

David's words hit her right in the gut. She tried not
to flinch. "Your father doesn't mention our interview in
this note."

David rolled his eyes in exasperation. "You were the
final nail in his coffin! Of course he was distraught when
he understood what he'd done to those coffee beans.
Obviously that was a mistake on his part—he's been getting more confused daily—but he killed his own daughter,
for Chrissake. It took us an hour to calm him down, Saturday night. And then you—"

"He'd been forgetting that Nora was dead for days,"
Merry interrupted. "He forgot she was even here in May.
Why do you think he remembered the fact that she was

poisoned—and possibly by himself—and felt bad enough to kill himself?"

"Because you dredged it all up," David said. "You made him vulnerable, questioning his escape from Laos."

"He never refers to our conversation about that in this note. And yet it was more recent than the conversation he overheard Saturday night."

David shrugged. "I don't pretend to understand the human brain. Talk to Andre about it. He's the psych expert."

"I will. I'd like to know whether he thinks Mr. Murphy was capable of remembering, even episodically, *that Nora's death occurred*. And capable of feeling personal responsibility for it." Merry raised the sheet of notebook paper. "Or whether he needed this cheat sheet to do that. Did you suggest he write down these words—*David says I poisoned Nora?*"

David Murphy frowned. "No. He must have done that Saturday night—right after he overheard us in the hall."

"After you'd spent an hour calming him down. He wrote about it in a notebook."

"Yes."

"How did you calm him down, Mr. Murphy?"

"With a shot of brandy and a Benadryl. I wanted him to sleep."

"And did he?"

"I suppose." David was increasingly annoyed. "I don't quite see what you're after, Detective."

"The state of your father's mind. Did he mention Nora's poisoning at any time yesterday? During Sunday dinner, perhaps?"

"Not to me."

"And yet, with his poor memory, he knew he had this phrase written in his notebook, tore it out, and left it on his desk as a farewell, before committing suicide."

"If he'd already decided to end his life," David countered, "he would never tell us. He wouldn't want us to stop him, once he made up his mind."

"—If he could do that," Merry persisted. *"Make up his mind."*

They were both silent an instant, assessing each other.

"The truth remains," David concluded, "that he left that sheet of paper propped on his typewriter for one of us to find—along with his body."

"I'm not sure any of us know the truth about your father," Merry said.

Chapter Fourteen

WHEN THE AMBULANCE carrying Spencer Murphy had pulled out of the crushed quahog-shell drive, Laney said to Andre, "Dad's going to talk about the funerals now, I know it. And if he does, I'm going to scream."

She was leaning against one side of the doorway, while he propped up the other. They had both felt the need to watch the gurney slide into the cavernous mouth of the truck, schooled by the precise hands of the EMTs. It seemed wrong to let Spence go with strangers. The others hadn't been able to face it. Or hadn't bothered. Andre wasn't sure which.

"I should call Roseline," he said. "She should know. Before she hears it on the news."

"Dad's been talking about that, too," Laney said. "How Grandpa's a reporting icon. How his death will have to be 'managed' for the public. How we should expect calls from reporters. He's sitting at the dining room table with his laptop open, drafting a press release."

"I know it makes you crazy," Andre said gently. "But Dave's right. *The New York Times* will be all over this. Spence won a Pulitzer for them, back in the day."

"Because of Laos," Laney said. "Because of his story of torture and survival and death. I read it—*In the Cage of the Pathet Lao*. It was on the syllabus of one of my college classes. It's a horrible story, but I was really proud of the way he told it, you know? He said once that he rewrote and rewrote the text to make sure it was free of self-pity. He wanted the brutality to move people. That, and the fact that he could forgive his captors."

"That's what made the movie so powerful," Andre said. "Forgiveness. I wish I'd talked to him more about his work."

Laney shivered suddenly, although the day was warm. "Last night he said something weird. That he'd made money off a lot of lies. Do you think he could have had . . . some sort of PTSD?"

Andre frowned. "If he did, I never saw it."

"Wasn't he hallucinating when he was found Friday night?"

"I think that was probably due to his dementia. What's on your mind, Lane?"

"I've just been wondering lately if Grandpa was sort of . . . trapped by that book," she said slowly. "People expected him to stand for things he never really chose. Things that just happened to him. Like human rights. And authentic journalism. He wasn't allowed to just be a guy who liked bumming around the world with a camera telling stories anymore."

"That's different from post-traumatic stress," Andre pointed out.

"I know," she said unwillingly. "I've been looking for the reason he ended up alone on an island. Isolated from everybody. Living in his version of the past. Maybe he really was scarred. And that's why he killed himself."

"You believe he did that?"

"Don't you?"

"Of course not," Andre said.

"HELLO, MEREDITH. DID you get soaked by hoses this morning?"

Ralph Waldo was lounging on the cedar deck behind the Folger house on Tattle Court, well within view of his vegetable garden, a straw hat on his head and a glass of iced tea at his elbow. It was a few minutes past two o'clock. Spencer Murphy was lying in a steel drawer in the tiny Nantucket Cottage Hospital morgue. Clarence Strangerfield was attempting to lift fingerprints from a sheet of notebook paper that might or might not be a suicide note. He had found no marks of impact or bloodstains on the railings of the staircase below Step Above.

Joe Potts and Nat Coffin were still searching for a boulder capable of killing someone, buried in the scrub.

Merry had been on her way back to the police station when, on impulse, she had cut from Orange Street over to Fair in search of a wiser chief than Bob Pocock. She was on the verge of tears, the careful control she had maintained in front of the Murphys crumbling like sand under a rogue wave. *Did I drive Spencer Murphy to suicide?*

A fragile man roughly Ralph Waldo's age, who had probably loved his kids and grandchildren as much as Ralph did—who had lived a tumultuous life, and probably made mistakes, some of which he had buried under lies. A confused and fading man whose foibles would never be exposed to the world, now, because she— Meredith Folger, the embodiment of the Law—had triggered enough fear in his mind that he had thrown himself off a cliff.

Dear God. How would she live with herself?

She felt a spurt of anger toward Bob Pocock. *Shock tactics*, he'd said. Shock tactics. When she had told him that Nora's death was probably accidental. She should never have gone against her instincts about how to handle this case. What had she been thinking—that Pocock would value her work if only she did as she was told?

And the burden on her, now, and for weeks to come, would be this: she would never truly know if her questions about Laos had inspired Murphy's leap into death or not. Her effort to discredit his suicide note this morning was revealed, even to herself, as a pathetic attempt to avoid his sons' blame.

Confession was supposed to be good for the soul. Ralph was a Wharf Rat and Spence's friend. Would he absolve her?

"Spencer Murphy is dead," she said, pulling a bench from beneath the picnic table that dominated most of the deck. She had been catching splinters from this bench her entire life. It still needed sanding. "I'm sorry, Ralph. I know you liked him."

"What happened?" he asked. "Did his heart just give out?"

"He was found near the foot of his stairs down to Steps Beach," she said, "with a fractured skull."

"Was it an accident?"

"The family is arguing suicide."

Ralph's white brows shot up. "That's odd. Most people are at pains to prove exactly the opposite."

"I know. That's why I came to talk to you. His son thinks I drove Spence to kill himself."

Ralph rose from his seat. "Want some iced tea?"

"Love some."

He disappeared into the kitchen and reemerged a half-minute later with a glass and two pitchers grasped in a single large hand. "Brought some lemonade in case."

She mixed herself an Arnold Palmer and took a long draught. "Spence left a note on his desk that could be read as a farewell. I think the sons are hoping he killed himself because that explains two things—their father's death, and Nora's."

"The cyanide in the coffee," Ralph said. "They figure Spence was responsible for the mix-up."

"Yes. And if Spence thought or *knew* that was true—that he'd mixed up the coffee and the poisonous apricot seeds—he might have felt enormous guilt. And thrown himself off the cliff."

"I can see how that would settle the whole mess nicely for the rest of the Murphys," Ralph observed.

"Yes. It's tidy as hell. They can hold two funerals and send the police on their way."

"While divvying up a fortune. But you're not convinced? Is that why the son is blaming you?"

"David Murphy is furious because yesterday I sat down with Spence and asked him whether his book, *In the Cage of the Pathet Lao*, was based on a lie."

"Meredith! Of course it wasn't!"

"I have an outline on Nora Murphy's laptop that suggests otherwise."

Ralph stared at her. "But I remember when he escaped! It was on all the news!"

"Made a great story, didn't it?" She reached for more lemonade. "He won a Pulitzer for the *Times*, published a bestseller, sold the film rights. He must have made millions."

"He did," Ralph agreed. "And continued to write great books long after that. He wasn't a one-shot wonder."

"What if this first book—the whole survival story—was fiction?" Merry asked.

"I'd be shocked."

"And so would the rest of the world, who cared about the story."

"You mentioned an outline. For what?"

"An exposé Nora planned to write. She'd gone back to Laos and researched her parentage, Ralph. She figured out that her father was supposedly Spencer Murphy's Hmong interpreter, a man named Thaiv Haam, and her mother was his wife, Paj. Only there's a major problem with that. Nora was half-white. She was really Murphy's child. He may even have arranged the ambush that killed Thaiv in order to run off with Nora's mother."

"You mean, he was never taken prisoner by the Pathet Lao?"

"Not according to Nora."

"And you asked him about all this?"

"In front of his son. David Murphy asked to be present as his father's lawyer. Today he accused me of driving Spence to suicide."

Ralph looked as though his drink had turned sour. "Oh, Meredith. What a wretched situation."

"I'm sorry, Ralph. I should have known that with dementia like his, he wouldn't be able to answer my questions."

"With dementia like his, he ought to have forgotten them almost immediately," Ralph countered. "I'm sorry his son accused you like that. You were only doing your job."

"Thanks, Grandpa," Merry said. Her voice trembled slightly, but Ralph ignored it.

"Did Nora tell her father what she knew? And could she prove any of it?"

Merry shrugged. "We'll never know. The answers to both questions died with her."

"Oh, God," Ralph said suddenly. "Meredith—" He removed his gardening hat and twisted it unhappily in his hands. "If she *did* confront him, and he didn't want his past exposed—a sane man would have a motive for murder."

"Yes. How sane was Spence, Ralph?"

He sighed. "It varied. A month ago, he still knew John by name—but Friday morning when we ran into him at the Wharf Rats, Spence didn't recognize him at all. Once we were on the boat, he functioned perfectly well. He may have asked the same question once or twice. Acted like he'd never seen Tuckernuck before when we stopped to drop our lines. That's the upside of dementia, you know—the familiar world is constantly surprising."

"Trust you to find an upside."

"I have to, Meredith Abiah. I'm in my high eighties."

"A month ago, roughly, Nora disappeared," Merry mused, "and Spence's memory fragmented."

"A shock sometimes does that—precipitates a mental decline," Ralph said.

"The timing raises a question. Could he have been *pretending* to forget more in recent weeks, Ralph? Is it possible his memory—his confusion—wasn't as bad as Spence made them seem?"

"Dementia being a great storyteller's last lie?"

"And an alibi for murder."

"I'VE GOT THE clothes for your aunt Nora," Kate said to Laney as she entered the kitchen. "Would you help me pick out something for Grandpa?"

Laney was tossing a tiny ball for MacTavish, who was confined to the house while the police scoured the cliff face and examined Spence's bedroom. Andre had driven off with Elliot once the body was removed, saying baldly that they needed to get out of the house. She thought they were headed for Sconset, at the opposite end of the island, and a drink at the Summer House bar. David had issued his press release. Since the den was off-limits, he had made the dining room his command-central, taking reporters' calls there over his cell phone.

The official statement said only that Spence had died as the result of a fall. He was elderly enough that the cause of death would go unquestioned. It was for the police to determine accident or suicide, David said—and Elliot agreed that he was right. If the death was accidental, there would be fewer questions from reporters, less speculation online, and no need to mention that Spence's adopted daughter was dead, too. The suicide note need not be mentioned. It was enough that the family knew the truth.

David wanted the double funeral held as soon as possible at St. Paul's Episcopal Church, which his mother had always attended—she had managed the parish flower committee for years. Nora and Spence would be buried beside her in the peaceful old cemetery below Mill Hill. But there was no funeral home on Nantucket, which meant that Spence's body would have to be shipped by ferry to Cape Cod, prepared for burial, and shipped back, along with Nora's remains from the state lab in Bourne.

David had arranged for Nora's transferral from Bourne to a funeral home in Mashpee, which was sending a hearse and driver over to the island for Spence. The funerals could not be sooner than Friday, prolonging everyone's enforced stay on Nantucket.

And getting suitable clothes to the mortuary on the mainland was a sudden priority.

"Aunt Nora's being buried in that?" Laney asked.

Her mother was holding a pair of black leggings and a cotton top. "There wasn't much else but jeans in her luggage. She traveled light."

"Couldn't we buy her something more . . ."

"Laney. We don't have time. Help me with Grandpa."

She followed her mother down the hall to Spence's room. MacTavish tagged at her heels, his white head lifted toward the ball she still held in her hands. He was panting eagerly, oblivious to violent death, the only cheerful creature in the Murphy household. Laney stopped short. Spence's bedroom doorway was sealed with yellow crime scene tape.

"Damn," Kate said. "I forgot. I'll have to tell your father."

"We could go around," Laney said. "The French doors are open, aren't they?"

"There's yellow tape strung across."

"So I'll duck under it," Laney said reasonably. "We've got to get his clothes. The police will understand."

They retraced their steps and went out through the living room doors. Yesterday's gorgeous weather had given way to clouds and haze, although the July heat and humidity were just as strong. An oppressive day, Laney thought, that even the breeze off the ocean could not dispel.

"Grab Tav," Kate said urgently. "He's not supposed to be out here. They don't want him on the cliff."

Laney lifted the wriggling terrier around his middle and offered MacTavish the ball. He was content to hold it in his mouth as she ducked beneath the yellow crime scene tape that blocked Spence's open French doors.

The police had still not been in here; nor were they visible below the cliff. Still hunting for the boulder that had fractured Spence's skull, presumably. "If we hurry, they won't even know we were here."

Kate set down Nora's clothes on Spence's bed and opened the closet door. She began to shift through the hangers draped with garments. A few field vests. Some coats. "He has only six collared shirts, Lane. And look at this! The suit he wore to Nana Barb's funeral! It was twenty years old then."

She lifted the timeworn dark suit from the rod, shoving the rest of the clothes aside as she did so, and laid it on Spence's unmade bed. "You choose the shirt, sweetie."

Laney set down MacTavish and glanced into the closet. So few belongings, for such a long life. There was an upper shelf with boxes of photographic negatives stacked neatly, an ancient fedora, a camera case. Two more suits, equally old and too patterned for dignity. The six shirts. She fingered a striped one, held it out to the light.

"That works," Kate said. "Is there a tie?"

"Just a navy-blue one, with Nantucket Red whales on it."

"It'll have to do."

MacTavish gave a short bark and darted forward between Laney's legs. She grasped his tail, which was stiff as a poker, and pulled him back. He came dragging a black wingtip lace-up in his jaws.

"Thanks, Tav, that's exactly what we need," Laney said, and reached down to take the shoe from him.

"I remember these from Nana's funeral, too." She handed it to Kate. "We should bury him in his Sperrys. That's what he always wore. Without socks."

Kate, arrested, was staring at her hand. Laney's voice died away. Where her mother had grasped the shoe was a rusty smear, arcing from her thumb over her palm.

"Is that mud?"

Kate turned the wingtip over. The soles were clean. But now the stain had smeared both hands.

"No, Laney," she said. "It's blood."

Chapter Fifteen

"How soon will we know if it's Spencer Murphy's?" Merry asked Clarence Strangerfield.

"Depends on the lab. They're coming off a holiday weekend. Even if we request a rush, it could take several days."

The crime scene chief had been ready to call off the search for the nonexistent boulder that might have fractured Murphy's skull when Laney came pelting down the beach stairs, calling for the police. Clarence took the wingtip from Kate Murphy and pinged Merry on her cell phone. He understood immediately that the rules of engagement with the household had changed.

She and Clarence suited up in sterile jumpsuits and shower caps. They positioned Nat Coffin in front of the open French doors, barring access where tape alone had failed. He was ostensibly dusting doorknobs and jambs with black powder for latent fingerprints. Merry could hear David Murphy peppering him with questions—Kate or Laney must have summoned him from the dining room—but Nat was descended from people who had wielded harpoons in the South Pacific. He could handle a Boston lawyer.

Merry lay down on her side in front of the open closet

door, her face toward the French doors and her knees drawn up in a fetal position. "How tall was Spencer Murphy?"

"About six feet," Clarence said.

"And I'm five-ten. Would it work? If I'd been conked on the head and stored in the closet, would I bleed on those shoes?"

"A-yeh," Clarence said.

"And if his knees were drawn up—"

"—and riggah set in before the body was disposed of—"

"We know why we found him on the beach in that odd kneeling position."

Merry pushed herself to her feet. "Three hours, at the outside, Summer Hughes guessed, for the body to stiffen. We can assume Murphy was killed sometime after dinner and before midnight—then temporarily hidden, with his bedroom door locked from the inside and the murderer leaving by way of the French doors. Anybody who checked on him from inside the house would think Murphy was simply asleep, and leave him alone. Andre Henrissaint apparently did exactly that. Then, once the household was down for the night, the murderer came back through the French doors to carry the body out to the cliff and stage the suicide. Only the corpse was folded on itself. The rigor hadn't passed off by the time Murphy was discovered."

"Plausible," Clarence said. "Why didn't the murderah clean up the closet?"

"He did everything in the dark. It might have been risky to turn on the lights. He may not have realized Spencer Murphy's head was bleeding. The fractured skull probably seeped fluid slowly and then coagulated.

Otherwise we'd have found blood all over the closet. You know what head wounds are like—stuck pigs."

"Or maybe he mopped the floor and missed the shoes," Clarence said.

"Did the girl show you exactly where she found the wingtip?" Merry asked.

"It was the dahg," Clarence said, pointing to the closet's far left corner. "We'll have to exclude for canine saliva when we send in the evidence. I already took a sample from the pooch's mouth."

Trust Clare.

Merry studied the closet floor. There was the other wingtip, a pair of beat-up Sperrys, and a stained set of canvas tennis shoes. A pair of winter boots.

Clarence pointed out smears of blood on the boots and the deck shoes, as well as a dried stain in the corner of the closet's wooden floor. As Merry watched, he sprayed the remaining shoes and floor with lumisol—a compound that reacted to iron in hemoglobin—and shined a black light on the closet interior. The light revealed a concentrated area of blood stains on and around the shoes.

Clare shined the black-light torch on the carpet between the closet and French doors. No luminescence that might reveal blood. No telltale splotch that betrayed where Spencer Murphy was bludgeoned.

"If the blood congealed during the time the body lay in the closet," Clarence said, "there'd be no splatter when the murderah lifted him out to carry him across the room."

"I'm surprised the killer didn't check the closet in daylight."

"Maybe the granddaughter sounded the alarm too early," Clare suggested. "Anybody taking stuff from the closet this morning, when they were all supposed to be hunting for Murphy, would stick out like a sore thumb, don't you think?"

"—And then I taped off the entry," Merry said. "Do we assume Kate Murphy's hunt for funeral clothes was as innocent as she says?"

"If either of those women meant to clean up the closet," Clarence argued, "she'd have come in here alone. And she'd have lost the dahg."

Merry walked over to Nat Coffin, who was bent with an insufflator over the French doors. David Murphy had given up bullying him and gone away. "Did you find anything on the cliff face capable of crushing a skull?"

He glanced up. "Just a few broken beer bottles."

"Keep them for Clarence. He'll check them for blood and tissue."

"Unlikely," Clarence countered, "if the killah has a wit in his head."

"You think he tossed the murder weapon in the ocean?"

"Or somebody else's trash can, where we'd nevah think to look. There're a lot of roll-away construction dumpsters in this neck of the woods."

He was right.

"Then search them all."

Merry watched Clarence place the wingtips carefully in evidence bags. She could leave him to it; there were questions she needed to ask, and timetables she had to compile.

ALICE ABERNATHY HAD spent the July Fourth holiday in her preferred way. She had avoided town and its disruptive crowds entirely, heading out Milestone Road to the Old Sconset Golf Course. This was not the famous and breathtakingly expensive Sankaty Head, which abutted some of Old Sconset's holes and boasted Silicon Valley potentates among its numerous offshore members. This was the public course that straggled through the cranberry bogs and moors, with its neat parking lot roped off in nautical fashion, its snug and welcoming clubhouse with a working fireplace and bar, surrounded in summer by native perennials. A branch of the Coffin family had owned the land and run Old Sconset for much of the past fifty years, when it was known locally as "Skinner's," but they had aged and found that their children, who lived off-island, were not interested in golf. The land was sold to the Land Bank, which happily leased the course to a rival facility, and preserved as pristine open space what might have been transformed into one hundred housing lots.

Old Sconset offered only nine holes. It was a favorite of year-round islanders who loyally patronized the course in the off-season. Alice liked to play. But she was a terrible golfer, so she preferred to pull into the parking lot on days when nobody else would bother to stop at Old Sconset—like the Fourth of July—and wheel her bag behind her as she tackled the fairways alone.

After she had hacked her way through the ninth hole— a par four, and her last—for a total score of seventy-two, Alice loaded her clubs in the back of her Toyota RAV4 and drove the short distance down Milestone Road to the center of Sconset.

She could have ordered a drink at the golf course bar. But the Summer House was so lovely—so evocative of off-island wealth and glamorous lives—that she left her car on the grassy verge of Magnolia Avenue and walked up Ocean to the restaurant fronting the southern tip of the island and the Atlantic.

There were only two other people at the bar—one black, one white. The black man was arrestingly handsome and enviably dressed. *Like a model in a Hugo Boss ad,* Alice thought. Whereas the other one was so ordinary—a classic Irish-American of the sandy-haired variety. She averted her eyes from the pair of them, aware that she was staring. She spent too much time alone. It was a problem she'd intended to tackle during the summer months, when the island was less isolated, but somehow her taste for solitude persisted.

She ordered a French 75 and pulled out her cell phone. She pretended to scan texts while she listened to the two men.

"We can't just ask David to disclose the terms of the will immediately," the sandy-haired one was saying. "But we've got to have a detailed plan to present when he *does.* After the funeral, probably. If he's intending to sell the house now that Spence is gone . . ."

"He can't sell. We can't let him," the black man said tensely. "It's important to you, El. A big part of our future. Where we raise our kids."

Alice almost choked on her drink, she was so startled. That beautiful creature? With the Irish-American?

"Besides, you inherit half the house. Which means you have equal say in what happens to it."

"I can't buy Dave out. He knows that," the sandy-haired man said.

"You can't be sure. Only David knows how much

Spence was worth; you could be in line to inherit millions. Just wait and see before you catastrophize."

"He wants market value. And you know it needs work."

"Shit," the black man said. "Why can't he give us a break?"

"Because he's settling scores."

"I wish I brought in more money, El. I wish I weren't a constant drain on you."

"Don't," the sandy-haired man said. "Your work is more important than any inheritance."

From the corner of her eye, Alice watched the sandy-haired man press his partner's wrist. Their fingers clasped briefly; she felt a searing jolt of pain. To have that kind of connection, that kind of unspoken love—

"When he was still capable of planning," the black man said, "he talked about a scholarship fund. For a homeless kid who was good at writing. The Spencer Murphy Award for Journalistic Excellence. I bet David has never heard about it."

Alice tipped back her drink and set her glass carefully on the bar.

"Excuse me," she said. "But I couldn't help overhearing. Are you gentlemen saying that Spencer Murphy is *dead?*"

The sandy-haired man stared at her. "Yes. He died this morning. Why?"

Alice smiled at him tentatively and proffered her hand. "Alice Abernathy. I'm the lawyer who drafted his last will and testament a few weeks ago."

Chapter Sixteen

MERRY FOUND DAVID Murphy sitting at the dining room table with a legal pad in front of him and a cell phone in his hand.

"I'd like to ask a few questions, Mr. Murphy."

"I have one to ask *you*, first." David set down his phone. "When are you people going to finish here, and leave us in peace? We're grappling with a major family crisis, not to mention the demand for information from the journalism community. I have difficult and complex responses to formulate for the public. I can't believe the insensitivity of the Nantucket Police, trailing yellow crime scene tape all over the house—after the interrogation you conducted yesterday drove my father to suicide. We've limited the official statement of his death to *accident*, of course, but with evidence vans and police SUVs in the driveway, rumors are bound to fly all over the island. You've even delayed the process of my father's funeral, by refusing access to his *clothes*. I'll be drafting and filing a complaint with your chief, Detective. Suicide is horrible enough for a family to bear; but your incompetence, callousness, and ineptitude have destroyed our privacy, too."

"People with privacy concerns rarely give their cell phone numbers to the press." Merry pulled out a dining chair and sat down. She lifted her laptop onto the dining table and opened it deliberately. She had removed the sterile jumpsuit, gloves, booties, and shower cap she'd worn in Spencer Murphy's bedroom. It occurred to her that she was dressed inappropriately—in red shorts and a navy blue and white T-shirt dusted with rhinestone stars. Her Fourth of July Parade wear. The dunk tank and face painting booths of the morning seemed to have existed in another country.

David Murphy bared his teeth. "That's exactly the kind of remark that will get you fired."

Merry glanced at him over her laptop screen. "We have reason to believe your father was murdered, Mr. Murphy, sometime between last night's dinner and this morning's discovery of his body on Steps Beach. Could you tell me, please, when you last saw him?"

"Murdered?" he scoffed. "That's absurd. Nobody would kill Dad."

"Somebody did. And the working assumption is that he or she is staying in this house."

"Impossible. Do you know what you're saying?"

"That your father was killed by one of his family? Yes, I'm aware of the implications."

David reached for his cell phone. "I'm calling the police station right now and getting somebody out here who knows what they're doing. This is outrageous."

"Do you always browbeat people when you dislike what they say?"

"Yes," Kate Murphy interjected. "It's his worst habit. It rarely works. But he never seems to learn from his failures."

She was leaning in the doorway behind her ex-husband.

He turned his head and glared at her; but Kate did not drop her gaze. "I found blood in Spence's closet," she said.

David set down his cell phone. "What?"

"Or rather, the dog did. The police think it was from his head wound."

"But he died on the beach!"

"No," Meredith said, "it's probable he died in his bedroom, from a deliberate blow that fractured his skull, and was later carried down to the beach." Her eyes flicked to Kate Murphy's face. "Would you be available for a few quick questions in private after I've talked to Mr. Murphy?"

It was not really a request, and Kate understood it was also a temporary dismissal. "Of course," she said, and walked swiftly away from the dining room toward the stairs. Merry waited until she heard the woman's footsteps die away at the top of the steps. She had no desire to let Kate know her ex-husband was under suspicion.

"Now, would you tell me, please, Mr. Murphy, what time you last saw your father?"

"Around seven-forty-five," David said. Disbelief still warred with anger in his face. "He's been tiring early. Dinner seemed to exhaust him this weekend—too much conversation flying around the table that he couldn't track. I've gotten in the habit of walking him to his room as soon as the plates are cleared."

"How did he seem last night?"

David shrugged. "Confused. Tired. He asked the same question repeatedly—about some charity project he thought Kate and Andre were working on together. Which shows you how mixed-up he was. Andre's the charity guy. Kate just lives off her windfall from the divorce."

"How long did you stay with him?"

"About ten minutes at most. I helped him take off his shoes. Handed him his pajamas. Made sure he had a glass of water by his bed."

"What shoes was he wearing yesterday?"

"His Sperrys. They were the default pair."

"Did you leave them on the floor, or put them in his closet?"

"I honestly don't remember. Probably the floor."

"Did you two discuss anything else?"

"Not that I recall."

"How did you leave him?"

"He was sitting on the edge of the bed staring blankly into space. I said good night and closed the door, hoping he'd actually get into his pajamas and go to sleep."

"Unlike Saturday night, when he left his room and overheard you in the main hall."

"Yes. But it was impossible to watch him constantly," David said.

"You didn't consider locking him in his room?"

"The door locks from the inside." He was frowning now.

"You could have thrown the lock and left by the French doors."

"Which would then have been left open. Allowing him to wander . . . Ah." He had clearly discerned the trend of her questioning. "The bedroom door was locked this morning, wasn't it? And the French doors wide open. No, Detective, I didn't leave them that way."

"And once you'd put your father to bed?"

"I came back through the house, fixed myself a vodka tonic, and went up to my room to work."

"Roughly what time?"

"Say, eight o'clock. I stayed until Laney called up from the bottom of the steps that the fireworks were starting." He pursed his lips grudgingly. "She seemed to think I ought to watch."

"Any idea when that was?"

"Not really. A little after nine, I'd guess, but I honestly didn't look at the clock. I went out to the lawn and stood there until the fireworks were done."

"Was anyone else with you?"

"Everyone."

"Immediately? All at once? For the entire time?"

He knit his brows in an effort to remember. "It was dark, of course, and we were all looking out toward the sky over Jetties. I know Elliot was standing near me for a while. He told Andre to go get Dad—I asked him not to disturb him, but Andre disappeared into the house. When Elliot says jump, Andre asks how high."

"Your daughter? Her mother?"

"Kate was standing near Andre—they had plastic chairs but didn't bother sitting in them. Laney wasn't with us most of the time," he said. "I think she was hiding under the trellis arch, at the top of the beach steps."

"So even though she wanted you to see the fireworks, she didn't watch them herself?"

"She preferred to pout. I was there to be her audience."

Merry lifted her brows and waited.

"I suggested she move in here to take care of Dad. She didn't like the idea."

"Does she have training in caregiving?"

"How much experience do you need to live with your own grandfather?" he exclaimed. "It's not like she'd have to cook or keep house. Roseline would do that." The annoyance died out of his face. "Anyway—it doesn't matter now. She can go back to Boston and waste more of her life."

He'd given his daughter an implicit motive for murder. But he seemed unaware of that.

"Elliot probably told her to call me down for the fireworks," David added. "He has this thing about group activities. That's why he wanted to get Dad out on the lawn, too. He likes to sustain the illusion that we're one big happy family."

"But you're not?"

"Now that Dad's gone, I wonder if we'll ever bother to assemble again."

"How long were you outside?"

"Maybe half an hour."

This tallied with Merry's own sense of the Jetties fireworks program. "You were on the lawn the entire time?"

"Yes."

"No bathroom breaks or trips to the kitchen to refresh your drink?"

"I only had the one vodka tonic."

"And after the fireworks ended?" Merry asked.

"I went to bed. I read for a while. I put my light out when I heard Elliot and Andre come up the stairs. That was around eleven."

Merry's fingers stilled above her keyboard. "Did you hear any unusual noises during the night, Mr. Murphy? Either inside—or outside—the house?"

"None." He gave a half-smile, stifled as soon as it dawned. "I was dead to the world until Elliot knocked on my door, a little after eight this morning."

"You got up right away?"

"Immediately. He said Dad was missing. I told El I'd start walking toward town—I thought I might overtake Dad on foot. I figured he'd head for the Wharf Rats. But the clubhouse was closed. I went all through town, up and down Main and its cross streets, thinking Dad might be caught in the holiday crowds, but of course I didn't see him. By the time I got back here, Andre had found his body."

"And Elliot had discovered the supposed suicide note on the typewriter." Merry lifted her gaze from her laptop screen and studied David Murphy. "What do you make of that note, now we know that your father was murdered?"

David pressed his fingers wearily to his eyes. "I suppose he thought it would convince the police that Dad had killed himself."

"He? Who is *he*, Mr. Murphy?"

"The murderer. Whoever it is. I'm from a generation that still uses masculine generic pronouns."

"So you weren't suggesting that your brother, Elliot, killed your father?"

"Of course not," David said sharply.

"But you are suggesting that the note was deliberately torn out of the book and placed on the den typewriter as false evidence of suicide. That is one possibility; the other is that your father did this for reasons known only to himself. If the murderer left the note, how do you think he—or she—knew that Spencer had written that particular phrase in the notebook? Is anyone in your family in the habit of reading Spencer's diaries?"

"I haven't the faintest idea."

"Do you read them, sir?"

"No, Detective."

"Where are your brother and Mr. Henrissaint now, Mr. Murphy?"

"Out. Elliot's highly sensitive, Detective. Grief requires him to retreat to a trendy bar where he can drown his sorrow in fifteen-dollar cocktails."

"You might try his cell phone."

"It's on his charger in the kitchen. He wanted to be unreachable."

"Then would you locate your daughter for me?" Merry asked. "I'd like to talk to her outside, on the lawn."

SHE DELIBERATELY STOOD near the arched rose trellis that straddled the gate to the steps—where, if David Murphy was to be believed, his daughter had spent the duration of the fireworks show, staring down at the tangled growth that sprawled between the cliff and the dunes, where her grandfather's body was later found. Merry had left the living room's French doors open. Laney Murphy came through them and stopped short on the deck.

Merry turned and smiled at her.

Slowly, Laney crossed the unkempt lawn.

"You wanted to talk to me?"

"I did," Merry said. "Tell me about this morning. When did you get up?"

Laney blinked rapidly, hesitating. She had been expecting a different question, Merry thought. Something about a bloody shoe.

"I woke up around seven. Maybe a few minutes before, actually—like, six-fiftyish. I haven't been sleeping well here."

"Waking up during the night?"

"Kind of. Just really light-sleeping, you know? Like, aware that I'm just dozing while I dream. My mind is going constantly."

"And that's not how you usually are?"

"Not at all."

Merry waited. The girl did not disappoint her.

"I've been really creeped out," she said in a rush. "What with my aunt's body lying on the roof for, like, over a month and my dad saying that Grandpa poisoned her. *Accidentally*. With stuff I brought and left in the house! I mean, *Jesus*. Between us we killed her. And I didn't even know she existed!"

"Your parents never mentioned her?" Merry turned back toward the beach, staring out over the dunes to the harbor. No Peter knifing the waves today; she wondered with a pang what he'd been doing since she'd deserted him on Main Street this morning.

"I *know*, right? And my mom definitely *liked* her. I mean, my mom likes most people, she's not incredibly anal like Dad, but even Grandpa said so. *You're the only one who liked Nora besides me*. Weird, right? And then—" She stopped short.

"What?"

"Nothing," Laney said.

Something, Merry thought. "So yesterday morning you got up and came downstairs."

"Yeah. I like having this place to myself. Before everyone else is up. It's incredibly beautiful with the silence and the view of the ocean and the sun coming up over the town."

"Yes. You're lucky to be able to spend time here."

"I know. It's so unspoiled. Thank God the wind farm project died—can you *imagine* those turbines sitting right out there, an industrial plant in the middle of the Sound?"

"I think we'd have gotten used to it," Merry said. "On hazy days, they might have looked just like a ghost fleet. Turbines are probably inevitable at some point, you know. Clean energy."

"Maybe," Laney said uncertainly. "But it's our *view*. Grandpa hated the wind farm; he wrote editorials about it every year, in the *Inky Mirror*. Although now . . . I hope Dad sells Step Above. I really do. I think it's incredibly gross that people have died here. I'd never sleep. Would anybody want to buy a place where there have been bodies lying around, though?"

Merry glanced at her. "Most of the houses on this island are centuries old. Countless people have died in them."

"I *guess*. Right."

"What did you do when you got up?"

"*So.*" She drew a deep breath. "I made some green tea. Then I came out here to do some yoga—it's really centering for me, first thing in the morning, especially outdoors in the natural world. Plus, my muscles hurt from all the gardening we'd done. Pulling weeds really strains the hamstrings." She glanced over either shoulder, as though suddenly perplexed. "That's weird. The wheelbarrow's gone. And the shovel. I guess Dad must have put them away. We meant to use them today to compost, but then Grandpa changed everything."

"Okay," Merry said. "Roughly how long were you out here?"

"I wasn't," Laney explained. "I got outside, unrolled

my mat—my yoga mat—and saw Grandpa's doors wide open."

"The French doors to his bedroom."

"Yeah. I didn't want him coming out and disturbing me while I practiced, so I walked over to, just, you know, shut the doors—thinking he probably wasn't even in there—and he *wasn't*. So then I freaked out, because I know he's been wandering and I *knew* he hadn't been in the kitchen when I came down, because his coffeepot wasn't on the stove, so . . ."

"You went looking."

"I woke up Mom," she finished.

"Any idea what time this was?"

"Maybe seven-twenty."

"And then?" Merry asked.

"Mom searched a little, and then she and El woke up the rest of the house. Dad was really pissed off, because he *knows* Grandpa's been loose before and he thought somehow I should have stopped him—like I was even up when he left—"

"He was probably just mad at himself," Merry suggested. "Your grandfather already went missing once."

"Maybe," Laney said uncertainly. "Dad's always mad. That's why I was *not* about to move in here, like he wanted, to look after Grandpa. It'd just be an excuse for Dad to blame me all the time."

"You told him no?"

Laney flushed. "Not yet. But I was going to. It's just— I'm between jobs right now. I used to be with Teach for America but the conditions in my classroom were really unsafe and I decided not to go back after the first year. So I've been leading classes at a local center."

Merry wondered what Laney considered unsafe. Hot glue guns? Sharp scissors? Or sharper kids? "You're teaching yoga?"

"Yeah. And although he totally disapproves, Dad's basically supported me. *Financially.* Not emotionally. Which he suggested he was no longer going to do, if I didn't move in here with Spence."

"I see. Will your grandfather's death change that?"

Laney looked bewildered. "Well, it's not like he's going to need me here anymore. Even Dad can't make me live in an empty house."

"No—I meant, do you think your grandfather left you any money? That might allow you to be more independent?"

The girl's expression changed. Her eyes widened and a vivid expression of hope flooded across her face. "Omi-*god*," she said. "I never even *thought* of that. Do you think he really might have?"

"I have no idea. The possibility didn't occur to you?"

"Not in a million years," Laney said fervently.

So she hadn't killed him for her inheritance, Merry thought. Had she killed him to escape penal servitude on Nantucket?

"When did you last see your grandfather?"

"At dinner. Not that we really talked. Ever since I found out how Nora died . . . that Spence may have been responsible . . . it's been awkward." Laney hesitated. "And then there was this really weird thing that also gave me the creeps."

"At dinner?"

"Before. Spence was out here in his plastic chair while Mom and I grilled burgers and generally got dinner going—Dad is useless in the kitchen and Andre has been doing way too much, particularly when he's not even family yet."

"Yet?"

"He and Uncle El are getting married."

"Ah." Merry filed this away. Elliot's inheritance would eventually be joint property. "Your grandfather was out here?"

"Yes. Andre had mixed him a G&T, which was probably a mistake, because once he drank a little he started talking in this confused and rambling way. All about Aunt Nora and how she'd found out the truth."

Merry's hackles rose. *Careful*, she thought. "The truth?"

"About the past. That's what he said. Mom sent me into the kitchen and took away his drink. And he didn't bring it up again during dinner. But it got me thinking. That Aunt Nora had *threatened* him somehow. Everyone always talks about how close they were, but his voice was different last night. *Distant*. He was trying to think through something complicated. And he was doing it out loud. That was how his mind worked, lately—he verbalized his thought process. And you could hear how fragmented it was."

Laney was young, Merry thought, and less than articulate—but she wasn't stupid.

They were both silent a moment.

"Is that possible, Detective Folger? I mean . . . is it possible . . . that he killed Nora on *purpose*?"

"I think maybe you watch too much TV." Merry kept her voice light.

"My dad agrees with you." Laney smiled faintly. "I told him Grandpa had been talking about Nora. Dad brushed it off, but he went to see Grandpa after the fireworks were done. I think he was worried about him."

"Even though Andre had just checked on him?" Merry's interest was deliberately casual. David Murphy had never mentioned seeing his father after eight o'clock the previous night. Sometimes people told stupid lies to the police out of fear. Sometimes they were deliberately concealing evidence.

"Dad doesn't trust easily. He likes to handle things himself." Laney glanced over Merry's shoulder. "There's Andre now."

Chapter Seventeen

"YOUR DAD WANTS you inside," Andre said to Laney, "that is, if Detective Folger is done with her questions."

"Almost," Merry said. "When did you last see your grandfather, Laney?"

"When he left the dinner table last night. That was a little before eight o'clock."

"What did you do after dinner?"

"I walked down to Steps Beach with my mom. Got our toes wet. We really haven't had a beach day all weekend, although we thought about going to Surfside this afternoon. The blood in the closet changed all that."

Andre frowned, and glanced quickly from Merry to Laney. This was the first he'd heard of blood. Merry turned and started walking toward the house. Laney fell into step beside her. After an instant, Andre followed.

"Back to last night," Merry continued. "How long were you down by the water?"

"We walked almost to Dionis," Laney said unhappily. "I needed to talk to my mom about this idea of me moving in with Grandpa. She kept urging me not to rule it out too quickly. Which means, I guess, that she doesn't want me to live with her in Brooklyn, either."

"When did you get back to the house?" Merry asked.

"It was around eight-forty-five," Laney said. "I didn't have my phone with me, so I can't give you an exact time, but maybe Mom can. She and I separated at the staircase. I went upstairs to pee. I don't know what she did."

"And then?"

"I saw it was getting dark." She glanced over her shoulder at Andre. "You called up the stairs to say you were getting ready to watch the fireworks, and to tell my dad. So I did. I spoke to him through his bedroom door."

"Did he answer you?" Merry asked.

Laney hesitated. "I don't remember. I left it up to him whether he wanted to join us."

"Then you went downstairs yourself?"

"Yeah. But I didn't feel like hanging with everybody. I'd really counted on my mom taking my side. I just sat under the trellis and thought about . . . everything."

Andre reached out and shook Laney's shoulder slightly. "You'd be welcome to live with us. If we had another bedroom."

"Thanks, Dre."

They had reached the back deck. Merry turned. "One last thing. You said your father checked on your grandfather last night, after the fireworks. How do you know that?"

"I saw him walk down the hall to Spence's room as I went upstairs to bed. There's nothing else on that hall."

"You didn't talk to him?"

"Why would I? Dad's not my favorite person in the world." Comprehension dawned suddenly in her gray eyes. "Was he the last person to see Spence alive?"

"It's possible," Merry said carefully. She had no intention of sharing her suspicions with Laney. "Thank you. That's all I wanted to know."

The girl hurried into the house.

"Blood in the closet?" Andre said to Merry in an undertone. "What is she *talking* about?"

"It looks like Mr. Murphy was deliberately clubbed in his bedroom," Merry said, "hidden until after the rest of the house had gone to bed, then placed on the beach during the early hours of morning. We found blood that is probably Spencer Murphy's in his closet."

"You think this happened after dinner? Maybe during the fireworks?"

"That's what I'm trying to establish. You don't seem surprised."

"I'm not." Andre sat down on the brief steps that led from the back deck to the lawn. "Spence was too much of a survivor to commit suicide. But he was exactly the kind of guy to walk out into the dark on his own and accidentally die trying to reach the sea. I never considered murder."

"Would you answer a few questions, Mr. Henrissaint?"

"Of course. But please just call me Andre. Everyone does." He patted the step beside him. "Let's stay out here for a while. Neither of us is family. And a whole lot of shit is about to hit the Murphy fan."

Merry perched next to him. "Besides this murder investigation?"

"Oh, yes. Elliot and I brought a local lawyer home with us. She claims to have drafted Spence's will. Except that as far as we know, Spence's will was drafted by David, years ago. He's not going to be happy."

"I see. Did the woman say when she did this for Mr. Murphy?"

"In May. While Nora was here. Alice—that's her name, Alice Abernathy—actually met Nora."

Merry digested this in silence. There could be only one reason for Spencer Murphy to go behind his son's back and draft a new final testament: because he had changed the provisions of his will, and had no desire for David to know.

"How can I help you?" Andre asked.

She glanced at him. He looked, she thought, more strained than at any time in their brief acquaintance. It was probably a full-time job, managing Elliot Murphy's emotions.

"Could you run through your movements last night?"

"Starting when?"

"The end of dinner."

"Okay." He pressed his right forefinger and thumb to the bridge of his nose, as though resetting an internal switch. "The girls grilled burgers. It was a pretty quick meal—bread, salad, ice cream. Everybody was a little tense yesterday."

"Why?"

"Because of what happened Saturday night. Nobody wanted a repeat."

"When Mr. Murphy overheard his son discussing his daughter's death?"

"Spence was supposed to be in bed. So David was a little unguarded. He basically laid out for us what you'd told him and Laney Saturday afternoon—that Nora died because the apricot seeds were mixed up in her coffee beans. He said that Spence had probably confused the two bags and was responsible. It wasn't a good thing for his dad to overhear."

"What was Spence's reaction?"

"He was furious. Agonized. He almost attacked Dave, who wasn't the real problem—Spence was angry at himself. But it took a while to calm him down."

"I heard. Brandy and Benadryl."

"Right," Andre agreed. "Anyway—he never brought it up yesterday. Neither did anybody else. We were all out and about. But at dinner . . . Spence wasn't talking. He insisted on having a pre-dinner drink when all of us fixed them, which isn't the best thing for a guy with dementia, but hey—he was technically the weekend host and we were in his house. I gave him a weak G&T to keep him happy. But it definitely made him drowsy."

"You're a psychologist. How would you characterize his state of mind yesterday? Was he depressed, in your opinion?"

"Yes and no." Andre steepled his fingers like an academic. "Dementia of the Alzheimer's type usually begins in the hippocampus, which is also where geriatric insomnia and depression start. In fact, much of the research suggests that insomnia in the elderly—a byproduct of advanced age—triggers depression and, eventually, dementia. The moodiness is part of the decline. But was Spence unusually morose last night? No. That's why I didn't buy the idea of suicide. Particularly in response to a specific catalyst, such as guilt over Nora's accidental death. I think Spence forgot whatever he heard David say in the hall Saturday night."

Merry said nothing of her own interview with the dead man; for now, the explosive outline on Nora's laptop would be known only to David Murphy and herself.

"So in your opinion, his memory problems were real?"

she asked Andre. "Not just a convenient dodge by a clever man who didn't want to answer too many questions?"

It was the first time she'd put the question so bluntly to a member of the Murphy household.

"Oh, it was real," Andre assured her. "I watched his decline. I noticed a plunge in memory and mastery of life skills at least three months ago."

Three months ago. If Andre was correct, the decline predated Nora's arrival—and death. Long before Spencer Murphy had any need for a dementia alibi.

"Did it ever occur to you to suggest that Mr. Murphy be cognitively assessed?"

"All the time," Andre said. "But I'm not a medical doctor. I'm a PhD. David had his father's power of attorney—that was his decision to make. I'm not family."

As he had emphasized once before.

"Okay," Merry said. "So dinner ended. What did you do then?"

"The dishes," Andre said. "That's the deal. When the women cook, El and I clear and clean."

"Not David?"

"David doesn't do anything for Kate if he can help it. Or *with* Kate, for that matter. Which means he does nothing to contribute to the household. Except hold grim and threatening family meetings. As he's probably doing right now."

"You don't like him," Merry said.

"He takes after Barbara. So no, I can't say I love David. I'm pleasant to him. I make a point of being pleasant to assholes. It gives me a sense of moral superiority."

"Barbara," Merry mused. "She comes up a lot in

people's stories about this family. And yet never with a great deal of affection."

"Laney loved her. She must have been a good grandmother." Andre tore some brown grass from the untidy turf at his feet and shredded it between his fingers. "But I don't know that she was a great parent. Right up to her death, she was convinced that Elliot wasn't gay. That he was a *good boy* who'd somehow been corrupted. By New York. Or people like me—brown immigrant outsiders who have nothing to do with the real America. I was the degenerate in El's life. Barbara hated me for it."

"Did that create a rift between Elliot and his mother?"

"He was constantly trying to make her happy. Which I think she secretly liked. Disapproval gave her a hold over El. But if you asked him honestly—he knew she was a throwback to a different age. And something of a bigot."

"Yet she adopted a child from Southeast Asia."

"Spence did that." Andre looked at her directly. "Spence was totally different from his wife. That's why the boys are such opposites. Elliot is all feeling and empathy. David lives in a cage."

"You really don't like him."

"I've heard too much about the emotional and psychological damage Barbara did to Elliot. David wasn't much better." Andre smiled sadly. "It's an old story. A bad marriage that hurts all the kids, no matter how successful they look to the world. I have no idea why Spence and Barbara ever stayed together. She resented him, resented the entire adventurous life he lived without her, and she nursed a monumental grudge. That's what really killed her. Cancer was just a name the doctors finally gave to something that had been eating away at her for years."

Merry nodded once. This was not a description of her childhood—but she recognized something of Peter's family in Andre's words.

"How long did the dishes take?"

"Maybe fifteen minutes. After that El and I took Mac-Tavish for his evening walk—straight down Lincoln Circle toward town. There were a lot of parties going on behind the hedges. Cars everywhere. People had parked up here earlier in the day and walked down Cobblestone Hill to Jetties."

Merry understood; most of the streets leading directly into Jetties Beach were barricaded off on the Fourth of July, to encourage people to walk or take the public shuttle to the fireworks.

"We went as far as Cobblestone and stood at the top of the hill, staring out over the crowds for a little while. There was a band—we could hear it in the distance—and the light was fading in that lovely, gradual way it has in summer. A wind picked up. There were kids shrieking from the swings in the dunes. It was a relief just to see something *normal*, you know?"

"Yes," Merry said. "I do."

"But then it was getting dark and Elliot said, 'We should go back. We should watch the show from the back lawn."

"A family activity," Merry suggested.

"Right. He's big on that. Elliot cares more about the idea of family than any other Murphy. Which is kind of ironic. Because to have a family of his own—"

"He needs you," Merry said.

Andre looked at her wordlessly.

"Laney told me you're engaged to be married."

"That's true," he said.

"I'm getting married at the end of September."

"Congratulations," he said. "You're doing it here?"

"Yes. In the Congregational church on Centre Street. With a reception to follow in a family house on Cliff Road."

"To *die* for. We're thinking we may just go to City Hall."

Merry had a sudden vision of a tent with sea-blue flags and a parquet dance floor, Ralph waltzing down its center. "Don't," she urged. "It will mean so much to you later. If you honor your choices. Despite whatever Barbara may have said."

Andre's expression was questioning.

"I'm telling you this because the man I'm marrying has a mother who regards me as an interloper. Half of me wanted to run away rather than face her down and claim my prize. It doesn't matter. Honor the person you love. That takes courage—but so does life. You'll never regret going forward, instead of back, when it mattered."

"Okay," Andre said.

"Now." Merry recovered her impersonal tone. "What time was it when you got back to this house with your dog?"

Chapter Eighteen

PETER WAS CROSSING the lawn from the barn to the house when Merry drove in to Mason Farms. He grinned at her and waved. His expression was carefree, his long legs darkly tanned, and his movements loose with exercise and good health. Just looking at him, she felt a sharp sense of relief. Bob Pocock might expect charges and a case to back them up on his desk tomorrow morning, but for the next hour she was going to think only about herself.

He waited while she stepped out of her SUV, then leaned in to kiss her. His hand came up to cradle the back of her head, smooth her blonde hair. "You never changed your clothes. You've been at the Murphys all this time?"

"Yes. What did you do today?"

"I went fishing with John."

"No way!"

He laughed. "You sound so aggrieved!"

"I'd have given anything to be out on the water. Where did he take you?"

"Great Point Light."

This was the most isolated of Nantucket's three lighthouses, a white tower that punctuated the far-flung barrier beach that formed the northern arm of the island.

Tourists hired guides to drive them out over the sand to Great Point, which was a nature preserve; at the barrier beach's farthest tip, the waters of Nantucket Sound met the Atlantic in a cross-current rip that was treacherous to swimmers. It was also attractive to bluefish, however, which made it a good spot for throwing in a line. Merry was green with envy. The solitude at Great Point was unparalleled.

She walked with Peter into the house. She still kept her apartment over a garage in town, and spent most of her weeknights there, but this was supposed to be a holiday—and she had missed Peter. "You had a much better time than I did."

"And we're having bluefish for dinner."

"You actually caught something?"

He glanced at her witheringly. "I'm not that hopeless. Besides, your dad's a good teacher. And his boat is sweet."

"I wouldn't know."

"We'll get you out there." He handed her a glass of wine. "Now relax while I grill the fish."

Bluefish confounded most cooks who lived beyond the Atlantic coast. They were fierce ocean predators that fought hard for freedom once hooked on the line, and they yielded dark gray-brown fillets that had a distinctly oily smell and taste. They were best eaten the day they were caught. As a result, blues were only rarely shipped across country, where they sold poorly in markets. Locals knew that the fillets should be skinned, slathered with a mix of mayonnaise and lemon juice, and grilled over hot coals. Alternatively, they were wonderful smoked—and mixed with cream cheese and cognac to form pâté.

Peter didn't have to be told how to cook his fish. John

had filleted and skinned it on board his boat. Peter added minced shallots and fennel seeds to the lemon juice and mayonnaise mixture, spread it on the fillets, and draped them with thick slices of his own farm tomatoes. He wrapped the fillets in packets of tinfoil and set them on his grill rack. About ten minutes later, they would be ready to eat. He was serving them with potato salad and green beans.

Merry took a quick shower and threw on some loose summer pajamas.

Peter assessed her damp hair, clean skin, and comfortable clothing and said: "Your day was that bad?"

"It's definitely murder," Merry replied. "Could I have another glass of wine?"

SHE DIDN'T TALK about anything to do with Step Above while the two of them ate. The light faded over the cranberry bogs, Peter lit the candles in his deck lanterns, and they lingered as the night sounds of the moors crowded in with dusk.

"I have to write a report tonight," she said sadly.

"That is a tragedy." Peter lifted her plate. "You already know, then, who killed Spencer Murphy?"

She shook her head. "I have a good idea. But I have no proof. I'll make that clear when I hand Pocock my summary of the investigation to date. He asked for charges by tomorrow morning—but not even Pocock can order the impossible. I only realized I was dealing with murder this afternoon."

"The man's a little Hitler."

She glanced at Peter's face; it was carefully expressionless. "I know you think I should quit—"

"Not at all. I think you should have his job."

He disappeared into the kitchen. Merry stared after him, surprised. "I'm not qualified."

"That's bullshit, darling."

He was running water over the dishes, his attention entirely focused on the task at hand. She could see his silhouette through the kitchen window, neat and economic. He had never quite been so unequivocal in his support for her work before.

Peter reappeared with a mug of chamomile tea and handed it to Merry. "Want to tell me about it?"

"I'm struggling with the question of whether it's two murders or one," she said.

For now, her laptop was unnecessary. She would write it up more clearly once she had organized her thoughts.

"The other murder being Nora?" he said.

Merry nodded. "Spencer Murphy was definitely killed last night by someone staying in his house—most of whom are close family. He was bludgeoned in his bedroom sometime after dinner, temporarily stowed until the household was asleep, then carried out to be found near the foot of his beach steps this morning as though he'd accidentally or deliberately fallen to his death during the night, cracking his skull in the process."

"Which seems plausible enough. However—"

"We found blood on his closet floor. It's a safe assumption, pending lab reports, that it's Spence's."

"A careless mistake," Peter said.

"Correct. But here's the question: What if Spence was the intended victim *all along*? What if Nora's death—from coffee beans mistakenly mixed with poisonous dried apricot seeds—was a random error?"

"You mean, the self-grinding coffeemaker was deliberately set up to kill Spence? The first time he used it?"

"I can't discount that possibility. The alternative is that Nora died by mistake. Spence's family blamed *him* for the error—the mix-up between the two bags of beans and seeds. That theory made sense if the man was so lost in dementia that he walked off his own back cliff last night, or so consumed with guilt over his carelessness in Nora's death that he killed himself. But now that Spencer Murphy is a victim, too, I have to question everything."

"Starting with Nora's death."

"Exactly. If Spence was the intended victim when she died in May—and remember, none of the Murphy family admits to knowing Nora was even in the United States, so it's improbable she was deliberately murdered by one of them—it narrows the field."

"—To those who understood the self-grinding coffee machine and the cyanide contained in apricot seeds," Peter said. "Further narrowed, to those who had an opportunity to load the coffee machine here on Nantucket between Christmas and this weekend. With the expectation that Spence was bound to make coffee in the machine sometime over the winter or spring, when he was living alone."

"It's so nice not to have to explain the obvious to you," Merry said gratefully.

"That's a risky murder to attempt," Peter pointed out. "What if Roseline or any random visitor used the machine instead?"

"—As Nora did, in fact. It *was* a risk. But I think the murderer knew enough about the household's habits to take a chance. He or she knew Roseline never made the morning coffee. By the time the housekeeper arrived at ten A.M., both she and Spence had already consumed their breakfasts. The murderer didn't expect Spence to have overnight guests before the summer—which argues that the murderer is a close family member who understood Spence's schedule and life. He or she hoped Spence would run out of ground coffee in a can, try the new machine—or even better, have Roseline turn it on for him and thus incriminate herself if anyone asked questions. But ideally, there would never be a question of murder. There would be no autopsy. His death would be written off: an elderly man passing on from natural causes, no questions asked."

"They didn't figure on him getting coffee at the Wharf Rats instead," Peter observed.

"No. Or the habits of a lifetime. He liked his coffee perked. He never used the machine. Nora did."

"So who set them both up?"

Merry looked at him soberly. "I wish I knew."

"And why kill Spence at all?"

She hesitated. "One of two reasons. He was worth a lot of money. I don't know exactly how much—but I'm hoping to learn that from the lawyer who drafted his latest will. She agreed to meet with me early tomorrow, before she reads Spence's last testament to his family."

Peter did not react; he had no idea Alice Abernathy had exploded like a mortar in the middle of Step Above a few hours ago.

"And the second reason?" he said.

"Well—as I suggested this morning, Murphy's life was partly a lie. Nora intended to expose his Laos 'escape' as a fraud. Spence may have been too confused to understand the implications of that when she turned up here on Nantucket. Or he may have understood them very well. And seen Nora as a threat he was forced to kill."

"Was he mentally competent enough to rig her murder with those apricot seeds?"

Merry lifted her shoulders. "Not if his memory and confusion were authentic. I thought maybe he'd faked dementia to avoid a murder charge. A psychologist within the Murphy household told me Spence was truly tanking. Ralph said only that he'd gotten much worse since May, when Nora was here—which might have been a tactical ruse on Spence's part. But the fact that he was himself murdered last night complicates that idea."

"Because it seems unlikely there are two murderers— Spence and his own killer—working at Step Above."

"Statistically and psychologically. Yes."

"Statistically and psychologically, David Murphy is the most likely perp," Peter said. "He gave the coffee machine to his father. He bought and opened the bag of coffee beans. His daughter delivered the cyanide-laced apricot seeds. They were both last here at Christmas. He could have set up the coffee machine to take out his dad once he'd flown back to Boston."

"But that's so obvious it gives me pause."

Peter threw himself into a lounge chair. "You know the means. You know the opportunity. You even know a good deal about the motives. What you lack is a sense of the key players—the suspects in the case. Why exactly would one of them kill?"

"You played too much Clue as a kid."

"Winters were long in Connecticut. Entertainment scarce."

Merry sighed. And just then her cell phone rang.

She reached for it; the number was one she did not recognize. She almost let it go to voicemail—but then decided there was too much at stake. It might be one of the Murphys.

"Merry?"

"Who is this?" she asked.

"Cindy Ayers, over at Cape Air. You have a minute?"

"Of course." She had asked Cindy to check her passenger manifests, but in the chaos of this morning had completely forgotten to call her back.

"You were looking for a David Murphy, out of Boston."

"That's right."

"I can't help you."

"Ah," Merry said. So the lawyer had told the truth.

"There's no David Murphy out of Boston," Cindy said. "But I noticed there's a Kate Murphy, out of White Plains. That any use to you?"

"Kate Murphy," Merry repeated. "When did she travel?"

"Easter weekend."

"The end of March, early April?"

"The last weekend in March. She came in on a Friday, went back Sunday morning."

"Thank you, Cindy," Merry said fervently. "I'll get an actual warrant to you in the morning—I need your records as evidence."

"Just one thing."

"Yes?" Merry asked.

"You want to know anything about her travel record?"

"What do you mean?"

"Who accompanied her on the flight. She paid for both tickets."

"Of course," Merry said.

"It's a tongue twister," Cindy cautioned. "You may want to write it down. Passenger by the name of Andre Henrissaint."

Chapter Nineteen

MERRY AWOKE TO the distant sound of Sankaty Light's foghorn braying at intervals across an island plunged suddenly into mist.

Nantucket's nickname was The Gray Lady, with good reason. When the sun disappeared, the familiar landscape was shrouded beneath a shifting, opaque cloud. Bright summer color was oddly muted. The wet shingles that sheathed the exteriors of nearly every building darkened to sodden charcoal. The sea turned from marine blue to gunmetal. The air turned chilly. Vacationers, dressed in vivid slickers or sweatshirts stamped with Oversand Vehicle Permits, shifted from the beaches to the antiques shops and bookstores. For much of the off-season, Nantucket looked like this—monochrome and slightly bedraggled, just like the seagulls that huddled on wharf pilings, beaks turned into the wind. Summer People might lament bad weather, but islanders found it almost comforting. It reminded them that one day soon the hordes would retreat back across the Sound, parking lots would empty, and Nantucket would belong to them again.

Merry inhaled two mugs of coffee and drove straight into town without stopping at the police station. Alice Abernathy had told her she'd be available at 8 A.M.

The small house on Union Street glowed with lamp-light behind its sheer white curtains. The yellow gleam was comforting on such a dismal day—like the smell of hot soup in a nor'easter, Merry thought. She hesitated on the sidewalk. There were two paths to separate doors—one led to the house, the other to a discreet sign that read *Office*. She chose the latter. The door was unlocked; when she thrust it open, a bell rang. The waiting room just beyond the threshold was small, snugly furnished, and empty.

Merry waited in front of an untenanted reception desk.

"Detective Folger?" called a voice from an inner room. Alice Abernathy appeared in the doorway. "Joan never arrives until nine-thirty. Please, come in."

Merry followed her. The lawyer's private office was at the rear of the house—with a bay window overlooking a neat garden. There was a love seat nestled into the space; Alice gestured for her to sit there, and placed herself in a wing chair set at an angle to the window. She had traded her golf clothes for a dark blue pencil skirt and white blouse. She also wore very high heels. The additional inches lent an air of authority that had been lacking in cleats.

"May I offer you coffee? Water?"

"Nothing for me, thank you."

"Then tell me how I can help."

"As you've probably realized, I'm investigating the recent deaths at Step Above."

"Deaths?"

"Spencer Murphy's daughter, Nora, also passed away a few weeks ago."

Surprise and disbelief crossed the lawyer's face. "How bizarre. She seemed in good health. What happened?"

"We're not sure," Merry said carefully. "Ms. Murphy was poisoned—but whether deliberately or accidentally, we haven't determined."

"I see. Spencer Murphy's death was definitely accidental, though? The result of a fall, his son said?"

"I'm afraid it's a case of murder."

Alice frowned at her. "Was it random?"

"I don't think so."

"Then you won't be sharing details until you've arrested the person responsible," Alice concluded. "I'm glad you told me, Detective. I'm about to open my office to the Murphy family, and if one of them is a killer— forewarned is forearmed."

"I understand Spencer Murphy asked you to draft his will."

"Yes."

"When was that, exactly?"

"The third week in May. He came here to my office on a Friday afternoon—the twentieth, I think—with his daughter."

"How did he seem?"

"Was he competent, do you mean?" Alice smiled grimly. "I got that question yesterday, from the elder son. I wasn't surprised. I left Boston thirteen years ago when I came around the Point"—this was a local's phrase for moving onto Nantucket—"but I haven't forgotten David Murphy's reputation."

"Which is?"

"Precise. Uncompromising. A tough negotiator. I didn't expect him to lead with a threat—but he must have been feeling vulnerable."

"Tell me about his father."

"Spencer. Yes." Alice smoothed her skirt over her knees, her thoughts turned inward to the recent past. "I get a wide range of clients on this island, Detective—and most of their concerns are chicken feed compared to an urban practice. Some are civil issues—estates, divorces, workmen's compensation. Others are petty crimes. DUIs, shoplifting. Domestic violence. Drug possession."

Merry nodded. That pretty much described the local crime blotter.

"Whenever I'm presented with an elderly client, I have to consider competence. Especially when the testator volunteers that he has another will extant and is changing his provisions. *Most particularly* when the elderly client is famous on several continents and a beloved local celebrity." Alice looked at Merry directly. "In my opinion, Spencer Murphy was competent to order his will. He arrived with a handwritten list of bequests he wanted included, and language he thought was important. He'd composed it carefully beforehand. He understood why he was in my office. He went through his list point by point. I noted down his bequests and copied his final statement carefully. The following Monday, he read over the printed draft and approved it. He signed a clean document approximately fifteen minutes later. And asked me to file the original with probate in the Nantucket County courthouse on Broad Street."

"Is that usual?" Merry asked.

"Not really. The client's lawyer or executor generally retains the original until the client's death, at which point the will is filed with the court. But Mr. Murphy was being cautious. On occasion, clients request a will's immediate filing for safekeeping purposes. It is sealed by law until the testator dies."

"What does that suggest to you, Ms. Abernathy?"

"That Spencer Murphy didn't trust his son."

"Thank you. That's very helpful. Does this will you drafted significantly alter David Murphy's inheritance?"

"I don't know the provisions of the previous will," Alice said.

Merry had to concede the point. "What was his daughter Nora's role in all this?"

Alice shrugged. "Driver, I think."

"He usually drove himself."

"Caretaker, then. She didn't speak much. She was simply watchful."

Nora must have been familiar with her father's list of final bequests; she may have helped him draft them. In which case, her work was done prior to arriving in Alice Abernathy's office. "You had no reason to think that she had influenced Murphy in any way?"

"Oh, she definitely influenced him."

"The Murphy sons suggest she spent most of her life trying to get the better of them. Did she pull it off in the end?"

"Given that she died first—I'd have to say no. Would you like to see the will?"

"May I?"

"Of course. You're investigating a murder."

The lawyer moved to her desk and unlocked a steel file drawer. "I'm going over the document with the family today. Initiating such a meeting seemed the best way to defuse David Murphy's shock and hostility. Because there's no question that the will in his possession is no longer enforceable."

"He mentioned that he had his father's power of attorney and was named as executor," Merry observed. "Could he fight this document?"

Alice returned to the wing chair, settling reading glasses on her nose. "He's welcome to try. But each of us has the right to overrule a previous will at any point in our lives—unless, of course, mental incompetence has been proved. David Murphy never had his father cognitively assessed or declared incompetent in court. So he hasn't a leg to stand on. I'm sure he knows that. He just threatened malpractice to see how easily I scare."

Alice handed Merry a dark green three-ring binder. "There's a lot of boilerplate language at the beginning that you can skip over. Mr. Murphy's personal statement is on the fifth page. The bequests and trust documents follow."

"Trust?" Merry scanned the paragraphs that stated Murphy's legal name and address, revoked all previous wills and codicils, and declared the present document to be his last will and testament. Then she flipped to the fifth page.

I am fully aware that this document represents a departure from the inheritance provisions I outlined in the past. I would like to offer my family an explanation—because it reflects, after many long years, a fundamental change of heart. I have lived for the past five decades with the knowledge that my happiness, well-being, success in my chosen career, and respected body of written work are based on lies. Worse, my long life in the public eye was predicated on betrayal, exploitation, and murder. I attempted to make amends for my sins with the adoption of Npauj Haam, legally known as Nora Murphy, at the death of her mother in Laos. Npauj Haam is my biological daughter, and in her search for the truth of her parentage she uncovered my lies as well. The substance of Nora's journalistic work (hereinafter known as "Laos Project,") shall be deemed authentic and the terms of its use mandated under this document, as follows:

That having earned more than ten million dollars from my deceptive practices over the course of a lifetime, I will inevitably bequeath blood money, criminally obtained, to my heirs;

That the aforementioned assets would be better spent in redressing the wrongs and injuries done to persons displaced around the world by war;

That after the execution of specified bequests, the residue of my Estate, including the value of all real property and financial assets, shall be held in Trust, for the establishment of a charitable foundation to be known as the Spencer Murphy Fund, as defined in the Attached Trust Documents;

That this duty being duly discharged at my Decease, Nora Murphy agrees never to release the Laos Project or otherwise acknowledge the circumstances of her birth and/or parentage, in any form, printed, oral, or digital, to the public;

That until my Decease, all supporting materials pursuant to Nora Murphy's Laos Project shall be safeguarded and secured by Alice Abernathy, Esq.;

At the time of my Decease and the execution of this Last Will and Testament, Nora Murphy authorizes Alice Abernathy, Esq., to destroy all materials pursuant to the Laos Project currently in her keeping.

Beneath this series of stipulations were two signature lines; Spencer Murphy and his daughter had each signed and dated one. The document was witnessed and notarized.

"She blackmailed him," Merry said.

"So I gather."

"But without a view to personal gain. She even lost the chance to publish a sensational story—the result of what may have been years of work."

"I wouldn't know about that. The materials Nora Murphy signed over to me are in sealed packets, deposited at the Pacific National Bank. I have no idea what those packets contain. Once the will has entered into probate, I will, of course, ensure that the contents are destroyed."

Merry suspected that David Murphy would fight Alice for control of his sister's research—but she saw no reason to voice what the lawyer must already know.

The bequests were fairly simple. Spencer Murphy had left his manuscripts and files to the Library of Congress. That he regarded them as useful to future historians struck Merry as somewhat delusional, but then she reflected that not *all* his bestsellers were necessarily compromised— merely the first, which had catapulted him to fame and established his journalistic reputation.

He had left a signed photograph of himself to the Wharf Rats, for placement on the clubhouse wall.

He had left his ancient Volvo to Laney, along with his notes on the birds of Nantucket, in three notebooks.

"So Step Above, and all his money, go to the charitable trust? The sons get nothing?"

"That was the deal. At present real estate and asset values . . . roughly thirty million. It's terrible, of course— but the alternative was a public burning at the hands of his daughter. I suppose he couldn't face that."

He had embarked on his deception a coward, Merry thought—and ended it that way.

"This will allowed Spencer Murphy to live in peace for

the remainder of his life," Alice added, "and ensured the truth would die with him. I suppose he thought it was a good bargain."

"Does the fact that Nora predeceased him negate their contract? She can't publish in any case, now."

"Mr. Murphy might have destroyed this testament, had he lived. But this remains his last will, and its trust provisions are perfectly enforceable. Nora Murphy never benefited from the trust directly, so her life or death cannot affect it."

"So who's supposed to run the foundation?" Merry flipped further through the binder to the section of the will that pertained to the charitable trust.

"Mr. Murphy's former daughter-in-law, Kate Murphy."

Merry frowned at Alice. "I'm surprised Nora would trust anyone even remotely connected to the Murphys. Why Kate?"

Alice smiled a little sadly. "She was a compromise candidate both Nora and Spencer could accept. Spencer thought it was important that a family foundation be represented by a member of the family. Nora didn't want her brothers to have any fiduciary or executive authority whatsoever. They are explicitly barred from the foundation board by the provisions of the trust. If Kate were still married to David, I'm sure she would never have been named."

"What happens to all this money if Kate declines to act—or dies?"

"I am authorized to conduct a search for a suitable nonprofit director, and all connection with the Murphy family ends."

The lawyer glanced at her watch. "And now, Detective,

I'm afraid I'm going to have to close our meeting. I expect the Murphys to arrive in ten minutes—and much as I'd love police protection until this will is probated—"

"Don't joke," Merry said. "Two people have died for it already."

Chapter Twenty

"SO THIRTY MILLION in assets and real estate were just stripped from two guys who thought they were going to inherit everything," Bob Pocock summarized. "Too bad, if one or both committed murder for it."

"We can only *assume* that David and Elliot Murphy were Spencer Murphy's heirs," Merry cautioned. "We haven't seen his previous will."

"And it's moot, anyway, because that will won't hold up." Pocock glanced up from her report. "*Cui bono?*" he said.

"I'm sorry?"

"Who benefits? Find out which of these guys needed the money most, Detective, and then build your case. Is the Boston lawyer's firm going under? Does he have a nasty online betting habit or pay a fortune each week in prostitution? What's his Achilles' heel, and why would he want his father dead sooner rather than later? Or is the queer from Manhattan with the chocolate Boy Toy looking for a way to retire early? Maybe real estate isn't keeping him in cocaine in the manner to which he's become accustomed. Maybe the Boy Toy wanted to walk, to a guy with deeper pockets. *Cui bono*. Track that, and you'll track your killer."

Merry opened her mouth to explain that it was a bit more complicated than that—and then decided to save her breath. Pocock had worked in a city with one of the highest murder rates in the United States. He had seen organized crime hits, contract killings, gang initiation shootings, and every sort of death pact under the sun. She wasn't going to convince him that the obvious course was not the only one.

"Yes, sir," she said, and barely counted to eighteen, this time, before she was dismissed.

Now that the holiday was over, Howie Seitz was off beach blockade and able to assist Merry in her investigation. She told him to run credit checks on all the Murphys, including Kate and Laney. Howie liked this sort of background work, combing databases and search engines for pieces of a puzzle. Merry had learned over the past several years that she could rely on his results.

Back in her own office, she glanced at her watch. It was important to interview David Murphy immediately after he left Alice Abernathy's briefing, before his probable shock and anger about the will had completely faded. She judged that the lawyer would keep them until 10 A.M., and it was only nine-fifteen.

Nora Murphy's laptop was resting on her desk. She opened it.

Merry was no longer interested in the book outline or the few passages Nora had managed to draft. She was looking for something else: evidence of a hidden relationship. She clicked on Nora's email icon and opened her inbox.

She had found David Murphy's contact email address online through his law firm website, and had done a

similar search for Elliot's through his real estate company. Merry ran a search for any correspondence between
Nora and her brothers. She came up blank. If Nora had
informed either of them that she was returning home, she
hadn't used their professional email addresses. Merry next
ran a search for the brothers' first names, to see whether
any hits surfaced within the bodies of messages sent and
received. And there, she found what she was looking
for—only not in the way she expected.

There were numerous Davids referenced in a slew of
emails Merry quickly dismissed as contacts in Asia and
elsewhere, stretching back over nearly three years. But
since January, only one David was mentioned in Nora's
email correspondence—in a message she'd sent to Kate
Murphy.

Whose personal email address, surprisingly, was not
her name—but grayhairedgrrl@gmail.com.

Merry opened it.

Dear Kate—

*You were so thoughtful to reach out last year through
Facebook when Barbara died. Even if it was too late
for me to fly home for the funeral, it was helpful to
read your family news and your description of the
service on Nantucket. Of all the places I've loved and
left, Step Above is the one I miss most.*

*I've moved back to New York. I see from your
profile that you and David have parted ways, and
you're in Brooklyn. If you'd like to meet for coffee or
a drink, let me know.*

Nora

Merry scrolled forward from January. Kate had answered Nora. The two had met. And they appeared to have formed a friendship. The emails became less formal, less full of background and more functional—a vehicle for setting appointments and meeting places where the real conversations had taken place. They had probably communicated by text through Nora's phone, too, although Merry couldn't check that—Phil Potts had yet to circumvent its security controls.

The third Tuesday in May, Nora had sent an email that was merely a subject line of text—*Arrived*. Merry opened the attachment. It was a photograph: the view of Nantucket Harbor from Step Above's roof walk on an afternoon in late spring, when the tide was out and the dim shape of Whale Rock could just be discerned in the shallows beyond Steps Beach.

A view from the spot where Nora would die, a little over one week later.

Merry checked back through all the emails she had sent her former sister-in-law, and the answers Nora had received. She even checked Nora's trash file. But the email she had hoped to find wasn't there.

Kate Murphy had flown to Nantucket in March, presumably to see Spencer Murphy. But unless they had spoken about it face-to-face, Kate had never told Nora about the trip.

"Detective Folger?"

Jennie, a staffer who'd worked at the station for as long as Merry's father.

"There's a man asking for you at the desk. Andre Henrissaint. Want me to tell him you're busy?"

"No," Merry said quickly. "Thanks, Jen. I'll be right out."

~

"I TOOK THE island shuttle to the Rotary," he said. "Elliot drove everybody else to the lawyer's. Would you have time for a cup of coffee?"

Merry glanced at her watch. "I can give you twenty minutes. How about the Downyflake?"

There were several reasons to take Andre over to the institution on Sparks Avenue—there was plenty of parking; the Scotch Irish cake was unparalleled; and at this hour on a summer Tuesday morning, there'd even be a table. Most important in Merry's mind, however, was her duty to Bob Pocock. If the new chief demanded she eat lunch at her desk, she was damned if she'd have breakfast there, too.

"Oh, yeah," Andre said. "I have this thing about the Sconset omelet."

"Good. I'll be having ham, eggs, and baked beans. I recommend it on a rainy day."

"You forget: my girlish figure."

"—Which can easily bench-press twice my body weight," Merry said scathingly. "I'll drive."

They were lucky enough to nab a table in a corner, against a wall, where the din of morning breakfasters was lessened. Merry knew their server by sight—the Downyflake was a family-owned diner, and she'd grown up with half of them.

"Brian," she said. "Here's our order—but can we start with Scotch Irish and two coffees?"

"Of course, Mer. I'll bring some blueberry crumb cake, too."

"I've got to take some back for Elliot," Andre murmured,

"as a peace offering. He's going to be inconsolable when Alice is done."

"You know about the trust?"

He set down his menu. "In a manner of speaking. I didn't know that Spence had actually drafted a new will until we ran into Alice Abernathy last night. But I knew Nora intended to persuade him to do so. Kate told me as much, this weekend, after we'd found Nora's body. Elliot will be crushed that he loses the house. He loves Step Above more than anybody alive."

Merry's eyes narrowed. So Kate had known about the will and never mentioned it to her ex-husband. She wasn't surprised. Kate and Nora had probably worked out the terms of the trust between them, before Nora ever arrived on Nantucket.

She removed her watch and placed it on the table. Andre should know he was on the clock.

"So why are we here?"

"After you and I talked last night, and I understood it was murder, I thought you should have all the facts."

"—Or as many of them as you know."

"Elliot refuses to accept that one of us killed his father."

"But you don't have that problem."

Brian, the server, who had once eaten warm cookies in the Folger kitchen with her brother, Billy, after school, swooped down with a platter of Scotch Irish and blueberry crumb cake. He filled their mugs with scalding coffee. Without having to be told, he had brought a pitcher of steamed milk.

"My background was a little less sheltered than El's."

"Why did you fly here in March with Kate?" Merry asked.

He smiled suddenly. "You don't miss much, do you? Elliot had to show listings to a Russian oligarch all over Manhattan that weekend. I said I was spending it in Miami with family."

"You lied to him?"

"Yes." He met her gaze. "Kate wanted me to assess Spence's cognitive state. Unofficially. On Nora's behalf."

"You knew Nora was in the United States?"

"For the past few months, I've been serving as her private therapist."

Merry sighed and mixed steamed milk in her coffee. "You'd better start at the beginning."

"Kate asked me to have a drink sometime in February. I hadn't seen her in a while, so I took the subway to Brooklyn. Nora was with her."

"Why did Kate want you two to meet?"

"Nora was planning to confront her father about her adoption in Laos—she called it a necessary part of healing her abandonment issues. Kate thought that as a psychologist—and one who knew Spence—I might have some useful insights."

"And you were okay with that? It must have put you in an odd position with Elliot."

"It did. Nora explicitly asked me not to tell him I'd seen her. She wasn't ready to get back in touch yet. Her emotions were pretty volatile."

"What did she tell you about Laos?" Merry asked carefully.

"That her father's life was a lie." Andre served himself some blueberry crumb cake. "And that she planned to expose him with a book."

"And your advice?"

Andre lifted his hands in a gesture of futility. "Her Hmong mother . . . Spence . . . the man, Thaiv, who was married to her mother and died a horrible death—that happens in war zones all over."

"Huh. That's the best you could do?"

"Look, Detective—I've spent my professional life among the homeless," he said. "I've seen the pain of living on the streets. I told Nora that she was a product of American privilege, just like I am. That Spence hadn't been forced to adopt her and raise her in First World comfort. That she could have lived out her life as a half-Hmong, half-white orphan in Vientiane—and that her life there would probably have been short. That she didn't *know* Spence had deliberately betrayed her mother's husband to the Pathet Lao. That maybe he had done Nora a favor, in fact, by saving her mother's life. Maybe Spence was scared shitless when Thaiv was ambushed, and crossed the Mekong with Paj as fast as he could. And then dealt with the consequences—badly, very badly—afterward. Spence made some terrible mistakes. But he also tried to atone for them."

Merry stared at Andre. "He made a bloody fortune by fabricating his escape."

Andre shrugged. "Two wrongs don't make a right. Nora was willing to break a lot of lives. She was looking for some sort of psychological justice—and that meant publicly shaming a man she'd loved, the man who'd brought her into the world and eventually raised her well. I thought there were better ways to achieve *justice*. By urging Spence to help other people torn by war, like her family. She had the power to do that. I believe in speaking truth to power."

"Did she throw her drink in your face and walk away?"

"From that first meeting, yes."

Brian paused again at their table, dropping platters of eggs and omelets and baked beans and ham. Andre thanked him. "A few weeks later, Nora asked Kate for my contact info. And we met on our own. I hope I helped her come to terms with the past. Maybe the trust is evidence of that."

"You never told Elliot."

"No. She'd become a client. There were issues of confidentiality. And as you know, El was never one of Nora's fans. I thought I could keep my sessions with her separate. I thought when the time was right—when Nora reached a certain closure about the past, I could broker a meeting with El. He's not the person she thought. He was wounded by that family, too."

Elliot had insisted he hadn't seen Nora in ten years. "Did Nora ever meet with him?" Merry asked.

Andre shook his head. "She died before it was possible."

"Did you know that she was here in Nantucket, in May?"

"No. The last time I saw her was in April."

"Ah," Merry said. "After you'd flown here with Kate at Easter, and assessed Spence's cognitive function. You reported to Nora what you'd found."

"I told her Spence missed her. And that if she wanted to have an important conversation with him, she should do it sooner rather than later."

"You never mentioned that Easter trip when we talked last night."

"I did say that I'd noticed a decline three months ago. And that I'm not a medical doctor. I could only give Kate my personal opinion."

"She wanted to know whether Spencer was competent to change his will. In legal terms."

"Yes," Andre said.

"And you told her?"

"Yes."

"Andre," Merry attempted. "You urged Nora to set up a trust. To benefit victims like herself, displaced by war around the world. Did you know she'd convinced Spencer to appoint *Kate* to run it?"

From the stunned expression on Andre's face, this, at least, was news. He had been frank enough about everything else that Merry was convinced he wasn't faking.

"Kate? *She's* in charge?" He pushed aside his plate. "Jesus. It was supposed to be me."

Chapter Twenty-One

SHE DROVE ANDRE back to the house as soon as their meal was over. He talked little during the fifteen-minute drive, his gaze fixed on the rain beyond her Explorer's window, his fingers laced in his lap. Then, as Merry mounted Cobblestone Hill, he said, "A significant number of New York's homeless are refugees from war-torn places, Detective. I had planned to do a lot of good through Spence's foundation."

"Maybe you still can," Merry suggested. "You have a long relationship with the proposed director. She'll need places to put her funds."

Andre smiled. "And even if the director's agenda differs from mine—there are always ways to do good. I'll just have to be more creative, that's all."

Merry recognized that Andre had admitted a motive for Spencer Murphy's murder. He had expected to be named head of a charitable organization that would have raised the profile of his work among the homeless, and his professional reputation throughout New York City. Moreover, as foundation director he might have found a way to save Step Above from immediate sale—perhaps by defining it as an appreciable asset within the charity's endowment. Who knew what plans for the house he might have formed with Elliot, plans that might have lessened the sting of his partner's disinheritance? But none of that was possible, now.

Merry did not ask herself whether the genial Andre was capable of murder. In her experience, almost everyone was—provided the circumstances were enticing or threatening enough.

"They're back," he said as she pulled into the drive at 32 Lincoln. A black Audi was parked in front of the door. When Andre turned to thank her, Merry said, "I'd like to come in for a moment and talk to David Murphy. Would you be kind enough to tell him?"

"Of course."

She followed him into the house. "Thanks. I'll wait here in the hall."

The Westie, MacTavish, ran frisking to greet Andre and stood on his hind legs to busk Merry's knee. She rubbed his shaggy head. She had visited the place enough that he recognized her scent; in Tav's mind, she was a friend. Few of the other occupants of the house would view her that way.

Andre went in search of David. Merry released the dog and walked over to the main stairs. They were one of the oldest features of the house, straight and steeply pitched with no landing. Laney had said that she could see her father walking down the back hallway to Spence's bedroom Sunday night from the steps. She hadn't lied. The doorway to Spence's office was visible from the third step when Merry mounted it. There, the back hallway made a sharp turn and David would have disappeared from view as Laney went up the stairs.

The dog was still at Merry's feet, and with his head

cocked, was inviting her to follow him to the second
floor. She led Tav back to the doorway and rubbed his
chest.

"Morning," David Murphy said.

He had come from the kitchen. His expression was
as shuttered as usual, no more nor less. If the provisions of the will had shocked or angered him, he had
mastered his emotions. David would make a formidable adversary in court, Merry decided; he gave nothing
away.

"I'd like to talk to you privately about the disposition of your father's estate. Perhaps in his office?"

"Certainly."

He led her to the small room and sat, as he had once
before, in Spencer's chair. She drew a side chair up to
the desk and opened her laptop.

"I met with Alice Abernathy this morning. She
explained your father's will."

"I see."

"Could you tell me, please, in what way the present
document differs from the will you previously drew up
for him?"

"I'm not sure it matters. That document is now
moot."

"Unless you decide to fight the new one in court."
Merry smiled at him over her computer screen. "And
given that a number of you in this household cannot
have known that your father had a new will on the
night he was killed, the previous document is very
much a part of this murder investigation. People have
been known to kill for an expected inheritance—
whether they receive it or not."

David sighed. "The will in my possession—the one I was prepared to execute—had very different provisions. There was no trust, no establishment of a foundation. My father's assets and this house were to be divided equally between Elliot and me."

"And the value of those assets?"

David hesitated. "Well, my valuation of the house is only a guess. Maybe fifteen million, solely because of the lot. The structure's not in great shape. Anyone buying the place would raze or renovate it."

Merry shuddered inwardly at the thought of the battles either would entail with the historic preservation board. "You planned to sell?"

"I did. Elliot wanted to keep the house—I told him he'd have to buy me out."

Families, Merry reflected, had been destroyed for less.

"And the value of the rest of your father's estate?"

"That fluctuates, according to market," David said vaguely.

"Where are those assets at present, Mr. Murphy? Invested? In a bank?"

"Both."

He was plainly uninterested in sharing financial information.

"Alice Abernathy suggested the estate could be worth as much as thirty million, altogether."

"I'm not sure where she got that figure."

"From Spencer, I would assume."

"But as we know," David said, "his mind was failing."

"Which is one reason you had power of attorney," Merry added helpfully. "So that you could handle his accounts. Pay his bills. Did you handle his investments, too?"

"Why do you feel compelled to ask, Detective? You're investigating my father's murder, not his financial health. He was an old man. He'd lived a long time on his laurels. He had made money, sure—but he'd spent it, too. The taxes on this house alone are killing. And he was hurt by the economic downturn in 2008."

Merry clicked on her screen. She was looking for the email summary of the Murphy background checks Howie Seitz had sent her forty-five minutes ago, while she was happily eating at the Downyflake. "A lot of us suffered in the downturn. Let's talk about Cape Wind."

"I'm sorry?" David said, startled.

"Cape Wind. The private development company whose goal was to construct the first major wind farm off the United States, here in Nantucket Sound. It ran into some snags."

"It did. What has that got to do with my father?"

"You tell me, David." Merry looked at him blandly. "Most of the two billion in financing Cape Wind needed was from major underwriters—the Bank of Tokyo, a Danish pension fund, a Dutch private equity firm. You're a securities lawyer. You're not Cape Wind's lawyer—but you knew people there."

"I know many people in a professional capacity all over the country."

"Exactly." Merry nodded, as though he were a star pupil. "You organized a consortium—a group of twelve individual investors who pooled their funds. You sank a lot of that fund—something close to fifty million all told—into Cape Wind. You thought clean energy was the future and that wind power was inevitable in Massachusetts, where there are no fossil fuels to speak of and natural gas is expensive as hell. You wanted to be in on the ground floor. But then the downturn hit, didn't it? Cape Wind stalled during the recession; clean energy was a nice idea, but less of a state or federal priority when people were out of work and tax dollars were tight. Your consortium lost money. Some of the investors were clients. Some were friends. One was your brother, Elliot."

David didn't speak. He was sitting very still in his chair.

"You must have been thrilled, a few years ago, when it looked like Cape Wind was turning around—that they'd get the green light to start construction."

"I was," he said.

"Is that when you stole money from your father, in the hope of earning back your investors' stake?"

"I didn't—it wasn't—"

"Stealing," Merry finished. "It was *borrowing*, right? Against your own future inheritance? And no one would even know, once the return from Cape Wind came in. Spence would live for years. You'd have time to put it all back. With interest."

David cleared his throat. The sound was painful, as though years of emotion had hardened in his larynx. "It wasn't borrowing. Or stealing. It was *investing*. I had the authority to invest Spence's funds."

"In something he would never have approved? Your daughter told me he hated the wind farm project. It was going to ruin his view. He wrote editorials going back for years, in the *Inky Mirror*. Am I wrong?"

"You're not wrong. Dad lived in the past. He wasn't a business man."

"Unlike you."

David's eyelids flickered. "It was totally unforeseen that the major energy companies would walk away from their contracts to buy Cape Wind's product. Or that the legislature would kill the wind farm. Or bar Cape Wind from bidding on future projects. Nobody could have known."

"Nobody could have known that Spence would draft a new will, either," Merry said. "One more question, David. When you checked on your father after the fireworks Sunday night, was he dead or alive?"

KATE MURPHY HAD parted from the others as they walked out of Alice Abernathy's office. It was impossible to get into the car with David and Elliot; she would walk by herself back to the house. She needed time alone, to hug the copy of the trust documents Alice had given her close against her rain jacket. She had felt David's rage flaring along the brick sidewalk behind her like a rippling flame. She could still see the abyss of shock that had opened in Elliot's face as he'd listened to the lawyer's calm explanation that he could expect nothing from his father. She could not combat either David's anger or Elliot's questions right now. Even the bewildered Laney must wait until later.

I should get on a plane for New York tonight, she thought. *Get away from all of them before they destroy me.*

But for a few moments she wanted to glory in her surprise and giddiness entirely by herself. Only it would be nice, she thought, if she could share her joy with someone. Maybe Laney—but Laney would want to talk about *David,* and how impossible he would be to live with, now. She would be drowning in anxiety. Andre would be happy for her, of course, but it would be awkward to talk at Step Above. His attention would be on Elliot.

The image of Nora's face as she had last seen her—raising a glass to toast them both in Brooklyn a few months before—rose for an instant in Kate's mind. She closed her eyes and whispered to the shimmering ghost: *Thank you.*

She would definitely leave for New York tonight.

When she opened her eyes, she realized that she was entirely alone on Union Street and that the rain had increased. She hurried toward town, water splashing from the wet bricks into her flat shoes, the manila envelope full of papers shielded inside her jacket. By the time she reached Main Street her gray hair was dark and streaming with wet. She ducked hurriedly into the Fog Island Café and bought a large hot coffee.

Then she opened the file and began to study her inheritance.

WHEN MERRY WALKED out to her car, she found Laney sitting on the front steps, waiting for her.

"Any idea where your mom is?" she asked the girl.

"She wanted to walk home from the lawyer's. She said she needed time alone."

"I see." Merry handed Laney her card. "Please give her this when she gets back, and ask her to call."

Laney stood up and dusted the seat of her pants.

There had never been a moment since they'd met, Merry thought, when the girl hadn't looked worried. "Can I talk to you for a minute?"

"Sure."

"It's about my mom, actually . . ."

Chapter Twenty-Two

WHEN ANDRE WALKED through the door and saw Elliot's face, he knew that he needed to get him out of the house as soon as possible. He grabbed the leash and snapped it onto MacTavish's collar. "Come on," he said. "The rain's not that bad. You can talk while we walk."

"He'll get filthy," Elliot said despairingly of the white dog.

"He likes baths." Andre tossed Elliot his tennis windbreaker. Elliot zipped it without further protest.

They headed away from the beach, out Indian Avenue to Sherburne Turnpike, their chins tucked into their collars and their eyes on the ground. From there they could ramble with the dog, almost entirely undisturbed, among the backroads off Sherburne Way. Tav sauntered along happily, his hindquarters swinging, his nose thrust into every clump and tussock he encountered.

"Have you eaten anything today?" Andre asked.

Elliot shook his head.

"I brought some Scotch Irish cake back from the Downyflake."

"I can't believe you sought out the police," Elliot muttered. "What were you thinking? Why did you do it? You know how biased they are against black men—"

"I thought I should tell them that I'd met Nora," Andre said, "and got to know her in New York. Kate put me in touch with her."

Elliot's feet slowed. Andre kept walking, in pace with Tav.

"You met Nora?" Elliot repeated.

"Yes."

"And never told me."

"Yes," Andre said. "I was hoping eventually to repair the relationship between you two. But she died before it could happen."

He looked over his shoulder. Elliot was standing dead still on the road's wet verge, the latest shock of the weekend all over his face. Andre walked deliberately back to him.

"I'm ready to talk about it now," he said, "if you're ready to listen."

CLARENCE STRANGERFIELD WAS used to being damp. He had grown up in Siasconset sixty years ago, when the island in general and particularly that village had been virtually deserted after August. His father had put him on a boat before he could walk, and had taught him to scallop in the Coatue bends during the November commercial season—Coatue still had shellfish in those days before Brown Tide—with a chain mesh dragging net off the boat's stern. Sometimes young Clarence had hunted for bay scallops on his own, after school, wearing his father's waders that came up to his armpits and carrying a long, stocking-hat-shaped scallop net. The boys—it was always boys, except for Nellie Wilson, who had four brothers and never had a choice in the matter—picked them up one by one in rubber-gloved hands. On those days they waded in Madaket, riding out to the western end of the island on their bicycles, even in the rain. Sometimes they took out their pocket knives and shucked the scallops while still standing in the water, eating them raw.

So a brief summer shower or three didn't bother Clarence. Particularly in July, when the heat and mugginess were sometimes oppressive. What bothered Clarence was standing on his aching feet while Nat Coffin dumpster-dove through the roll-off construction waste bins that they were forced to search for Spencer Murphy's instrument of death. They had been at it for most of the morning, the construction dumpsters being full of such things as scraps of wood flooring, scraps of insulation, scraps of drywall and demo'd tile, ancient toilets and rolls of carpeting, various local residents' plastic and lavender-scented dog-poop bags they had hurled into the dumpsters while walking at night, other people's picture frames and old cartons and pizza boxes and paint cans—myriad, mostly empty, paint cans, which were technically toxic waste required to be recycled—tossed opportunistically into the dumpsters. The construction bins were the standard size generally in use on Nantucket—fifteen cubic yards. But they were microcosms of disposable American culture, Clarence thought, and of the quiet rebellion of island residents—who were so restricted in their garbage disposal that tossing a contraband item in any available receptacle was a secret pleasure.

Nantucket had faced a choice in the late '90s: organize around the stink of the town dump, which was noxious and alienating residents within a five-mile radius of its location along Madaket Road; or pay through the nose to ship all of the island's garbage—*all* of its garbage!—across the Sound to Cape Cod. The Selectmen had opted, in typical New England fashion, to support the environment and the future. Now 91 percent of the island's waste was recycled, processed as compost in the anaerobic digester, or buried in a strictly monitored landfill. But that meant everyone—resident and summer tourist alike—had to tediously separate their garbage into three distinct bins: Compost, Recyclables, and Landfill. It drove many Nantucketers nuts. Particularly the ones who flew in to rent someone else's house for two weeks each year, and saw no reason to get with the program.

"Hey, Clare," Nat Coffin said.

He was braced on a pile of refuse inside the final construction roll-off they'd targeted. It was the largest they'd dealt with, about forty cubic yards, Clarence guessed. It was positioned in front of a massive foundation cut into the sand above Steps Beach, the whole lot already terraced for multiple levels of dwelling, the native vegetation stripped and the soil nothing more than a wet and sandy slash on the face of the cliff. The dumpster sat right near the conjunction of Lincoln Ave and Lincoln Circle, closer to town than Step Above.

"Ayeh?" Clarence said.

Nat lifted a garden shovel in his latex-gloved hands. Clarence reached for it gingerly with his. The shovel was spade-shaped, not square-edged, and the apex of the tip was stained rusty brown. Clarence squinted and examined it narrowly. There were still a few silver hairs stuck to the steel.

"Well, I'll be," he said.

"Wait," Nat cautioned. "There's more."

And, grunting, lifted an ancient garden wheelbarrow over the dumpster's rim.

"I WAS TRYING to spare you pain," Andre concluded, as the two of them walked back up Indian Avenue toward Lincoln Circle. "You earned a lot of scars in this family. However much you loved Barbara, your relationship was always complicated. Spence was your hero. I couldn't let Nora destroy that. If I could persuade her not to publish . . . to channel her anger into good somehow . . . the foundation seemed ideal."

"But the house," Elliot attempted.

"I thought maybe we could put in an offer. Buy it from the trust." He hadn't told Elliot that he'd expected to be running it. That was a private wound Elliot didn't need to hear right now. "We still could. Maybe Kate'll cut us a better deal than David ever would."

Elliot lifted his shoulders despairingly. "Nothing seems worth it anymore, with Spence dead. Everything's over."

"Even us?"

They reached Lincoln Circle. Tav started to pull toward Step Above's drive. But Andre came to a halt on the circle's grass oval. There was a question he needed to ask before they entered the claustrophobic world of Step Above.

"Can you forgive me, El? For not telling you about Nora?"

Elliot looked at him, aghast. "After all you've done for me? Of *course*. You were just trying to protect me, Dre. You always do. You love me better than anyone in the world. I wish Dad had understood that."

He reached for Andre. The two men embraced, the dog sitting at their feet.

It was as he held Elliot that Andre saw the two men in the distance, lifting the wheelbarrow out of the roll-off dumpster.

KATE MURPHY HAD prolonged her time in town after her first cup of coffee at Fog Island. She had mastered the contents of the trust documents and had begun to make notes on a pad she kept in her substantial purse. There were so many tasks to consider, to list, to organize. She would first need a timetable for securing the foundation's assets; that would depend entirely on the speed of probate court and how well David, as executor, cooperated with the process. She would have to file the necessary forms to secure federal tax-exempt status. Consider the location of her offices—the number of staff she would need—how large her board should be and whom she should request to sit on it. She ran through various names in her mind, aware that she had no expertise in refugee-related issues and that she would need advice. Should the foundation concentrate on women and children—reflecting Nora's experience and legacy? Or should it be gender-neutral? Should it consider assistance for any regions of the world, or concentrate on the worst affected by war? Or were those areas already flooded with aid groups? Maybe she should concentrate on areas the world seemed to over-look. Maybe . . .

Overwhelmed, Kate stopped writing.

Or maybe Andre could help her get her arms around this job.

He had so much knowledge, so many contacts. He should be her first appointment to the board. She would ask him to help her.

That would have to wait, however, until they were all back in New York and could work around Elliot. She had always liked him—but she knew how deep his sense of disappointment and resentment must be. He must feel betrayed. He would demand explanations—so would David. Had she known Nora was in the States? Had she conspired to defraud them? All questions neither man had asked in Alice Abernathy's office. Kate was dreading them.

She should leave Nantucket as soon as possible. She couldn't imagine living in the house for the rest of the week while the others prepared for Spence's funeral. She would go back to Step Above now, and pack her bag.

Her cell phone trilled; she glanced at the text. It was from Laney.

Mom. Where R U?

Kate considered this. She almost didn't answer her daughter. Then she thought: *Forget the bag. There's nothing at the house you can't replace.* And texted Laney, *On my way to the airport, sweetie. Be in touch soon.*

Chapter Twenty-Three

IT HAD BEEN a long time since David Murphy had handwritten a personal note. The pen felt awkward in his hand, his fingers cramped. But his laptop was useless now; his father had never adjusted to computers, so there was no printer in Spence's office. David could have placed the sheet of paper in the ancient typewriter and tapped out the words, but he would probably have riddled the text with typos. He wanted his final communication to be error-free. And there was an intimacy—an authenticity—to handwriting. No one would question that David had authored his farewell.

It was only a few sentences long; all his life he had been concise and efficient. When he had signed and dated it, he sighed, rubbed his eyes, and left it propped on the typewriter. Just like the note his father had supposedly left.

The detective would note the similarity in method, of course. It would feed her assumptions, echo her theory. David took comfort from that.

He did not look back as he left the den, and he did not close the door.

Step Above was completely quiet.

He strode purposefully to the kitchen and opened the

cupboard. The bag of bitter apricot seeds still sat, half-empty, on the shelf.

David began to make coffee.

MERRY FOUND KATE Murphy sitting in the middle of the airport at Ackerman Field, waiting for the 2:48 Cape Air flight to White Plains. Nantucket's terminal was, relatively speaking, tiny. There was only one gate—a door leading out to the windy tarmac—and an old-fashioned stainless steel bin with louvered doors set into the wall, where baggage handlers dropped bags as carelessly as fast-food burgers. This was locally known as the "Arrivals Area." At the Departures end of the terminal, the security scan was set up immediately in front of the exit door. There was no maze for passengers to navigate; few flights out of Nantucket were large enough to require them. The rest of the terminal consisted of a couple of airline ticket counters, a pair of rental car agencies, a place to buy coffee, and a kiosk that sold postcards and water and T-shirts with whales on them.

Also, an ATM.

There were a number of flights to White Plains each day, but on a Tuesday immediately following Fourth of July weekend, Merry's desperate hope was that they were booked, and Kate Murphy would be forced to cool her heels. She left her police SUV brazenly in the tow-away zone in front of the terminal (it was only two cars long), and her hope was rewarded. She spotted Kate as soon as she walked through the entrance.

"Just the person I wanted to see," she said affably as she took the chair next to Kate's. "Your daughter told me you were here. She's a little worried about you. She packed up your stuff before I left Step Above so I could bring it to you."

Merry set Kate's suitcase at her feet.

"I'm sorry," the woman blurted out. "I couldn't face them. David and Elliot. Even Laney. All those questions—"

"I can imagine. Your lawyer explained the trust to me this morning. Congratulations. You'll have a salary to count on, now. When's your flight?"

Kate told her.

"Well, that would have been nice," Merry sighed. "To be back in New York for dinner. But you realize you're fleeing an active murder investigation? One in which you're . . . actually a suspect?"

Kate stared at her woodenly.

"I'm going to have to forbid you to leave Nantucket," Merry said regretfully. "I can probably arrange for you to get a refund—the Cape Air folks are old friends. In the meantime, would you answer some questions?"

"Right here?"

Merry glanced around. "This has to be preferable to going back to Step Above, right? At least you can be honest. None of your family is listening."

"Of course. What do you want to know?" Kate asked.

"I'd like your comment on something, first." Merry pulled her cell phone out of her purse and opened her email. "One of my assistants sent me notes about your divorce settlement. I gather you left your husband under something of a cloud. You had an affair, isn't that right? With one of your daughter's college friends?"

Kate frowned. "How did you know that?"

"Divorce papers," Merry said briefly. "Public record.

David used that to screw you to the wall. He didn't have to divide his property, and because Laney's of age, he didn't have to pay child support. You received a settlement of two hundred thousand dollars—which, while nothing to sneeze at, is hardly what you might have expected from a man of David's supposed worth. You're renting your studio in Brooklyn, which isn't known for its economical rents, and you've yet to find a job."

"That's true."

"So this appointment you got today is something of a godsend. Did you know Spence had put you in charge of this trust?"

Kate shook her head. "I didn't even know there *was* a trust. Or a new will. I was completely surprised."

"Well," Merry temporized. "Not *completely*. You'd met Nora months ago. You knew she was going to propose something like this to her father. But you didn't know whether she'd had the chance to make it happen before she died. That's why you flew in here Saturday, isn't it? After Laney called to say that an aunt she'd never heard of had been found dead on Spence's roof walk?"

Kate frowned. "I flew here to support my daughter."

"That was a nice side-benefit, yes. When did you first see Nora in New York?"

Kate hesitated.

"Please don't lie out of a false instinct for self-preservation," Merry suggested. "The truth is easier to remember. That's important in a murder investigation."

"Nora contacted me in late January," Kate said. "She was flying in to talk to editors, and she'd realized from Facebook that I had left—that I had divorced David."

"Ah. I don't have her Facebook login. So I couldn't

access her Friends list or posts or messages. I was able to read her email, however."

Kate glanced at her swiftly. "You have Nora's laptop?"

"And her cell phone. Which is why I suggested you be as frank as possible from the get-go. I didn't realize, initially, that you were in contact with Nora right up to her death until I went back through her inbox this morning."

Kate's jaw clenched. It was a habit from years of suppressing comments she might have made to David in anger.

"Nora told you in late May that she'd arrived here, but she never emailed about her meeting with Alice, or her success in arranging the trust," Merry continued. "Didn't you wonder why she failed to answer your last message? Or the two messages you sent after that?"

"Of course. I tried her cell," Kate said. "But she didn't pick up. It went straight to voicemail."

"Must have made you nervous."

Kate shot her a quick glance. "A little. I wondered . . ."

". . . If she was cutting you off?"

"I thought maybe David had found out she was here." Kate's voice trailed away.

"Or maybe, that Andre had told Elliot everything," Merry suggested. "Not just that Nora was back in the States, but that he'd been counseling her to set up a trust. And Elliot could have alerted David. David could have flown to the island—"

"You know about Andre?"

"He came to see me this morning. He told me he'd been counseling Nora to channel her anger in useful ways. Confession is good for the soul. So as soon as you realized Nora was dead, you had to fly here. And see what was happening for yourself."

"It was so weird to hear she was lying up there, on the roof all those weeks," Kate said faintly. "I thought maybe Spence had snapped when she confronted him. That he couldn't deal with the threat of Nora's exposure. There was no other reason for why she'd died. She certainly *seemed* healthy. She was the farthest thing from suicidal. But when I got here, Spence was anything but angry. He was glad to see me. And then it was obvious the whole thing was an accident. He'd just mixed up the coffee beans and the apricot seeds—"

"You came because you needed to watch David, too," Merry added implacably. "You couldn't let David find out about the new will from a talkative Spence, and turn the whole situation around."

"I overreacted," Kate admitted. "Within hours of arriving, I realized Spence's mind was failing. He never mentioned Nora or her book. He'd forgotten she was ever there. He kept forgetting she was dead."

"Until Sunday night, right before dinner."

Kate looked confused.

"I mentioned that Laney was worried about you," Merry reminded her. "She's worried, specifically, that you somehow killed her aunt. An hour ago she told me that Sunday night, the night before he was murdered, Spence was talking more than usual. He'd had a drink and his mind was wandering. He was in one of his semi-lucid periods, in fact. He told Laney that Nora was going to write a book about the truth—but that you'd taken care of the problem. Or words to that effect."

"She said that?" Kate demanded.

"Yes. Laney saw you dump Spence's drink in the grass. She thought you were trying to silence him. It worried her enough that she persuaded you to take a walk along the beach with her before the fireworks so she could talk to you alone. Did she bring up Spence's ramblings?"

"Yes," Kate admitted. "I told her that her grandfather didn't know what he was saying anymore, but of course he hadn't meant that I'd *killed* Nora."

"He meant that with you running the trust, Nora was giving up on her book. But you couldn't mention the trust to Laney."

"No. Spence might have lived for years. It was utterly inappropriate to bring up his will before his death."

"And dangerous—you didn't want Laney to tell David about the trust. Spence might be dangerous, too, if he spilled the beans to either of the Murphy boys when you weren't looking. But you couldn't watch him *all* the time. You'd have to leave Nantucket at some point. Is that why you were such an advocate for moving Spence into full-time trained nursing care? On the mainland? In a professional facility?"

"I'm a former nurse," Kate lashed out. "I advocated for what was best for *Spence*."

"And urged Laney to consider moving in with him if David balked at a transfer to Boston or New York. That way, no one would wonder why you flew to Nantucket periodically to visit them. Laney wouldn't be much of a shield between Spence and David, but she'd be better than leaving Spence in the hands of people only David hired and paid. If Spence rambled more as he declined, David might learn from his paid caregivers about the new will. And take steps to persuade Spence to nullify it."

"That's a negative construction to put on what was a sincere wish for Spence's well-being," Kate retorted. "And why do you care about all of this, anyway? None of it matters, now. Spence is gone. David learned about the will today from the best possible source—his father's lawyer."

"What a relief," Merry said softly. "Is that why you killed him, Sunday night? To make sure he never talked again?"

Before Kate could speak, Merry's cell phone rang. She glanced at the screen. It was Clarence.

She took the call. And then said to Kate: "I'm going to have to ask you to return with me to Step Above."

She met Clarence where Lincoln Ave branched into Lincoln Circle, just south of the Murphy house, in front of a massive roll-off dumpster and a construction site. Laney was standing there; Merry had texted the girl to wait for them with the evidence team.

She and Kate got out of the police SUV.

"Mom," Laney said tearfully, and Kate went to her.

"I'm sorry, baby girl. I haven't been thinking clearly."

Merry was examining the treasures Nat Coffin had unearthed. The shovel was already encased in plastic. She turned to the two women. "Could I have your attention for a moment?" she asked. "Do either of you recognize these as belonging to Step Above?"

"Oh, yeah." Laney came forward. "I already looked at them while I was waiting for you and Mom. That's our shovel and wheelbarrow. It's so weird that you guys found them in the dumpster. Who'd throw away a perfectly good wheelbarrow? It had compost in it, too."

"When did you last see it, Laney?" Merry asked. She was concentrating on excluding Kate Murphy, so that the mother could not suppress the daughter's information.

"Sunday night. I put all the garden bags in Grandpa's car—I was going to drive them to the dump. Mom wanted to mulch the hydrangeas the next morning, but we never got to it because of Grandpa." She glanced at Nat Coffin, who was still standing in the dumpster. "Is there compost in there, too?"

"Hard to tell. Dirt's the norm, not the exception."

"Can you show me exactly where you left the wheelbarrow Sunday night, Laney?" Merry broke in.

"Sure," she said. "Mom?"

Without another word, Merry drove them both back to Step Above. Clarence waited for Nat to climb out of the roll-off, and followed in his evidence van.

When they arrived, Laney led them around the far side of the house. "That's Nana's compost pile," she said, pointing to the unruly heap of garden refuse decaying serenely under a beech tree. "You can see where I dug up the load from the bottom. I rolled the wheelbarrow around this side of the house to the backyard."

Merry and the others followed her along a path beaten into the turf, around the sagging wooden deck with its double sets of French doors—from Spence's bedroom and the living room—and the single door off the kitchen, near the barbecue. Laney was standing next to the semi-circular perennial beds filled with hydrangeas, punctuated in its middle by the rose trellis gate and plunge of beach steps. "I left the wheelbarrow right here. You can actually see where the metal supports sank into the turf. We'd watered the beds with a sprinkler at the end of the day, because we didn't know it was supposed to rain, and the wheelbarrow was heavy with compost."

"Was it still here after dinner?"

Laney nodded. "I almost tripped over it in the dark, after the fireworks."

"What about when you did yoga the next morning?"

Laney moved obediently to the spot where she must have spread her yoga mat, and stared at the perennial bed. After an instant she said, "It wasn't there."

"You're sure?"

"Positive. I remember thinking how nice Nana's coreopsis and phlox looked, now that the weeds were gone."

"Thank you for noticing, my dear," Kate said under her breath.

"And the wheelbarrow would have blocked my view of that clump," Laney finished, "where the two plants are grouped together."

"Thanks." Merry scanned the depressions in the ground where the wheelbarrow had rested. Both marks had visible divots—caused, she suspected, by shifting the heavy barrow out of the soft earth. Her face barely a foot above the ground, she made out the faint marks of a rubber wheel trailing through the unkempt grass. It was helpful that no one had mown it.

The trace disappeared at the trellis gate; of course, Merry thought—the entire world had been up and down those stairs in the thirty-six hours since Spencer Murphy's body was found at the bottom. Andre had gone down with the dog; the EMTs had gone down with a stretcher; Clarence and his boys had examined the treads and railings . . . and now steady rain had washed the stairs clean. She peered over the railing at each side. Then she reached down and grasped a fistful of soil.

"Does this look like your compost?" she asked as she walked back to Laney.

"Yeah. It's got that great, good-dirt smell," she said, putting her nose into Merry's palm.

"It was dumped down the cliff, to the left of the top step."

Laney frowned. "That's stupid."

Merry didn't bother to correct her. Kate wasn't even aware of them. She had turned her head, every fiber of her being listening; and Merry became aware that a small dog was howling somewhere close at hand.

And then she saw.

Andre was walking toward them across the lawn, with a single sheet of paper in his hand.

Chapter Twenty-Four

Dear Detective Folger,

You're correct that I'm facing financial ruin due to the misappropriation of both my investment consortium's funds and my father's assets. I therefore decided to kill my father, Spencer Murphy, on the night of July 3 in order to inherit his property. I thought I might be able to restore the money I owe to others, particularly my brother, Elliot, in part by selling my father's house at the peak of the market.

After the fireworks were concluded, I took a large wrench from the garage, went into my father's bedroom, and hit him over the head. I placed his body in the closet and locked the bedroom door. I exited by the French doors to the deck and returned to the house through the living room entrance. Later that night, I carried my father's body down to the beach and left it there. I threw the wrench into the ocean. And back at the house, I tore a page from his notebook that suggested a motive for suicide, and left it propped on his typewriter. On July 4, I made sure to be in town searching for my father at the time his body was discovered.

I am sorry for all the suffering I have caused,

particularly to Elliot, whom I have never treated as he deserved. I hope he can forgive me for the loss of his savings and the house, and that he finds happiness in his future life.

I can't face charges or prison—so I have taken my own way out. I hope Laney will forgive me.

I would like to be cremated, and my ashes scattered in the sea.

Merry and Clarence stared down at David Murphy's body. He was lying on his bed upstairs, an empty coffee mug on the bedside table. His usually pallid skin was tinged blue, a sign of low blood oxygen.

"Cyanide poisoning?" she asked.

Clarence held the empty mug under her nose. "You can still smell the apricots."

"Let's hope nobody feels the need for a cup of coffee right now."

"I already checked the coffeemaker, Marradith. He was good enough to empty the rest of the pot down the drain."

Elliot had taken the howling MacTavish away. He and Andre were sitting silently in the living room. Kate was still out back with Laney—the girl's horror at her father's death had found expression in hysterical sobbing, and she refused to come back inside the house.

"I'll call the Potts brothers and tell them we need divers off Steps Beach," Clarence said. "That wrench should have sunk to the bottom, and with Whale Rock blocking the tidal currents right at this spot, it won't have gone far."

"You won't find anything."

Clarence looked at her with something like sympathy. "But with this note on our hands and Pocock sitting in your father's chair, I've got to go through the motions. The chief'll expect nothing less. A signed confession is too tidy to ignahr. No charges, no arrest, no call to the district attorney—"

"How're you going to resolve that piece of paper with the blood and hair samples on the garden shovel?"

"Same as I always do," Clarence said. "Run my tests and let the evidence speak for itself. *You're* the one who has to write the report, Marradith, so's to make it all come out even."

She sighed. "I'll call for a medical examiner and ambulance, Clare. You deal with the Pottses. But ask them not to spread this around yet, okay?"

It was Dr. Fairborn, not Summer Hughes, who showed up with the EMTs from Nantucket Cottage Hospital. Summer was enjoying a well-earned day of freedom and Fairborn was enjoying a cigarette when Merry met him in the driveway. He stubbed it out before donning his sterile suit and booties. "Any chance the guy was offed?" he asked.

"No. But we'll need an autopsy all the same. You can fly him straight to Bourne whenever it's convenient. Remains to be cremated and returned to the family."

She left Fairborn to it. Then she walked around to the backyard, where Laney and Kate were sitting as far from the house as possible, side by side on the steps leading down to the beach. They turned and looked at Merry as she approached. Laney was composed now, although her face was blotchy from weeping.

"I'm sorry to disturb you," Merry said, "but I'd like to talk to you both. Preferably at the same time as I talk to Elliot and Andre. If you can't face joining them in the living room, Laney, tell me—and I'll ask them to come out here."

"No," the girl said. "I'm done being silly. I'll come inside. Mom promised we can get a hotel room for as long as we have to stay here."

Andre and Elliot were sitting together on the sofa with their dog between them. Tav lifted his head as Merry opened the French doors.

"Okay if we join you?"

"Of course," Andre said. "Laney, I'm so sorry."

"Can I have Tav?" she asked.

He lifted the Westie into her arms; she curled up in a wing chair with the dog in her lap and concentrated on stroking his head. Kate sat down opposite her daughter. Her expression was guarded.

Merry stood with her back to the fireplace and studied them all. "As you know," she said, "Mr. David Murphy is dead. It appears that he took his own life by poisoning himself with cyanide-laced coffee. I know that you are also aware that he left a signed confession to his father's murder. In it, he stated that he faced financial difficulties and killed Spencer Murphy in order to obtain his inheritance—not realizing that Spencer had drafted a later will that left his fortune elsewhere."

None of them spoke. They were waiting, passively, for her to tell them it was all over—that they could go back to their lives, forward into their futures, put the hideous weekend behind them. Case closed.

"I have a few ideas about David's note—why he'd have

written it, and why he took his own life. But I'd like to hear yours."

Elliot frowned slightly. "Isn't it obvious?"

Merry glanced at him. "Meaning?"

"He told us. He couldn't face prosecution."

"I agree that loomed large in his mind," Merry said, "but I think he wanted to avoid charges of fraud. Not murder."

"What do you mean?" Laney asked.

"Your father invested money for a group of people who trusted him, including your uncle Elliot. The investment lost money, so he took some of your grandfather's funds in an attempt to make things right—and ended up in a deeper hole."

"You mean—Spencer's assets, the ones that are supposed to fund the trust—are *gone*?" Kate interjected.

"Along with my life savings," Elliot said faintly.

"You'll still realize a huge amount from the sale of this house," Merry said to Kate. "Elliot, of course, is out of luck."

Elliot rubbed his forehead painfully with one hand.

"But that illustrates my point," Merry continued. "There was absolutely no reason for David Murphy to kill his father in order to inherit half his estate, as he might have done if the new will had never been drafted. It was in David's Murphy's interest, in fact, to keep his father *alive* as long as possible—so that his embezzlement of Spencer's assets went undetected. He was safe, so long as he remained executor and nobody asked questions about the disposition of Spencer's funds. Financial disaster only struck for David once Spencer was dead—and the will he'd drafted had to enter probate."

"That's true," Kate said.

Merry nodded at her. "You, on the other hand, had every financial reason to want Spencer gone as soon as possible."

"I loved—" Kate began.

"I don't doubt you did," Merry replied. "But I was speaking solely of financial motives. You had reason to believe that Nora had urged Spence to draft a second will, establishing a trust that you expected to administer. As I suggested this morning, that made any loose talk on Spence's part a potential risk—his mental confusion was deep enough that he might inadvertently tell David he'd disinherited him. You had a motive for silencing Spence and making sure his second will was never overturned—by killing him yourself. That became clear on Sunday night, right before the fireworks, when he told your daughter that *Nora won't write the book now, thanks to Kate.* He meant, of course, that Nora had agreed not to publish because he'd agreed to a charitable foundation you would run. If he'd said such things too often around David, your future, Kate, would have been at risk."

"I didn't know the second will had actually been written until after Spence was dead, and Alice Abernathy came to this house," Kate said quietly. "I would never have killed Spence with that kind of uncertainty. I might have been handing a fortune to my ex-husband."

"And I don't think you'd have taken Laney and the dog to sort through Spence's closet the day of his death, either, if you'd hidden his body there the night before," Merry agreed. "Even if you were unaware that his fractured skull had bled, you'd be foolish to bring witnesses.

It would have made far more sense to use the need for funeral clothes as an excuse to enter Spence's room *by yourself*, and clean up any traces of murder you had left behind."

"So . . ." Laney looked around the circle of faces. "Where does that leave us?"

"With Elliot," Merry said, "and Andre. Would you like to tell me what happened yourselves, or should I do it for you?"

The two men glanced at each other.

"El—" Andre said.

Elliot drew a deep breath. "It was me, Detective. It was me all along. Andre just tried to help."

MERRY ALLOWED PETER to feed her dinner that night. They met at Ventuno for deep-fried olives stuffed with pork sausage and braised lamb pasta and several glasses of Brunello. It had been, as she said, a very long day.

"So there was no wrench to find sunk in the waters off Steps Beach," Peter said.

"Because Elliot hit his father over the head with the garden spade Laney had left on the wheelbarrow."

"Why?"

"Fury." Merry toyed with her butterscotch budino. "Elliot had talked to David about the future on the morning of July third. He'd told his brother that he and Andre were getting married. And that it was his dream to keep the house on Steps Beach in the family. David wasn't enthused. He had his private reasons, of course— he needed to sell Step Above for as much as the market would bear, once his father died—but Elliot was frustrated that David wouldn't promise to cut him a deal, between brothers. So he went to his father that night, after the fireworks, and told him that David planned to unload Step Above. And that he, Elliot, meant to keep it safe—that he wanted to raise children there with Andre, and continue the Murphy tradition."

"And?"

"Spence had one of his odd mental turns. Dementia does that, apparently. He said something unforgiveable to Elliot about Andre's race. Or Elliot's orientation. Or both—I'm not sure, because Elliot wouldn't repeat his father's words this afternoon."

Peter furled his brows. Partly in pain, partly in sympathy. "It's always worse when it comes from your father."

"I know. I watched Spence do it to Andre once before, on Saturday morning. Andre was very forgiving. It helps, I think, that he's a psychologist—he can separate himself from people's behaviors, to a certain extent. He kept telling Elliot that it wasn't really Spence talking when he uttered ugly slurs. But Elliot insisted: *It has to be partly him. It came from his brain and from his mouth.*"

"But, Meredith, *killing* your father?"

"I'm not sure he meant to."

"He had to walk outside to go get that shovel. It wasn't an impulsive act."

"You just outlined the case for the prosecution," Merry admitted. "Elliot had seen the spade and wheelbarrow on the lawn during the fireworks. He ran out of his father's bedroom, grabbed the spade, and swung it at Spence's head."

Peter reached his spoon into her budino. "Where does Andre come in?"

"He woke up in the middle of the night and realized

Elliot wasn't in bed. So he went looking for him. He found Elliot pushing the wheelbarrow with his father's body in it across the lawn."

"So he helped him get Spence down to the beach."

"And then tossed the wheelbarrow and shovel into the dumpster. That was Andre's idea."

"It's odd, though," Peter mused. "You said that Andre and his dog discovered Spence's body, and Elliot found the fake 'suicide' note. Which he'd deliberately left on his father's typewriter."

"It's always worth a shot to try to look innocent. They hoped to convince us Spence had killed himself. Which was unfortunate, because it raised my antennae. Most grieving families would have been pushing the accident theory. Nobody likes a suicide in their midst."

"I hope your chief appreciates that. And your antennae."

"He was remarkably restrained this afternoon. In the best possible way."

"Well—you *did* get Pocock charges on the very day he'd asked."

Merry was quiet a moment, remembering how broken Elliot Murphy had looked as he entered the holding cell at the station. Andre had been placed in a separate one. He was talking soothingly to Elliot through the wall that separated them. Nobody, she reflected, truly understood the bond between two people—except themselves.

She spent slightly less than an hour drafting her report for Bob Pocock. He had kept her standing in front of his desk as he read swiftly through a printout.

"This is very . . . thorough," he said eventually. He set the pages on his desk and squared the corners with his fingertips. "A deceptively complex case, clearly laid out. The two victims—three if we count the suicide . . . the financial fraud, the discovery and significance of incriminating evidence . . . I have only one question, Detective, that you've failed to answer. Who killed Nora Murphy?"

"Her father," Merry replied. "Either he mixed the seeds and the coffee beans by accident, or he did it on purpose, and placed them in the machine."

"Although you maintain that this coffeemaker was too complicated for him to operate."

"It's possible he filled the cavity—then was flummoxed by what to do next. So he left the machine as it was, and promptly forgot about it."

"Or left it for his daughter to use, quite deliberately, the next morning. He might even have turned on the machine before leaving the house. Given himself an alibi in case her body was found immediately."

"He might have," Merry agreed. "But as we will never know, and cannot possibly prove it—"

"You don't suspect the housekeeper of eliminating a rival for her job?"

"Killing for a paycheck? There are too many openings on this island for a woman of Roseline's talents, sir. She'll have no trouble getting another position."

"And again, as we cannot possibly prove it—"

Merry was silent. She counted in her mind, and waited.

Pocock sat back in his chair and studied her. "Damn fine job, Detective, accomplished with commendable speed. You're a credit to this force."

"Thank you, sir."

She got to eight.

"You may go."

"And then there's David's suicide note," Peter said thoughtfully now as Ventuno's emptied around them. "What was *that* about?"

Merry pushed aside her dessert plate and sighed. "I think he found Spence's body on the night he was killed. David went to check on him after the fireworks, if you remember. He found the bedroom door locked—went around by the French doors on the deck—and discovered Spence in the closet."

"And he didn't yell?"

"No. He took counsel with himself."

Merry studied Peter soberly.

"David must have known someone in the household killed his father. I think David suspected it was Elliot. And when the second will surfaced, disinheriting them both, and he understood his own financial morass, he couldn't face the consequences. David tried to do something noble at the end—make up to Elliot for the loss of his savings and his loss of the family home. He shouldered the blame for Spence's death. In an odd way, he was trying to be the hero that Spence, as it happens, never was. He wanted Elliot to have a future—a happy one."

"That's fairly tragic," Peter said. "What do you think will happen to them?"

Merry leaned her head back against Ventuno's banquette. "I think a competent lawyer will argue provocation, and prove the attack was spur-of-the-moment. I think Elliot will get six-to-ten for second-degree murder. And I'm not sure Andre will wait for him. He's a lot younger. Elliot will be much older and poorer when he gets out."

"Meredith." Peter took her hand. "O, ye of little faith. Don't you know that real love abides all things?"

"Does it?" she asked.

"It does," he said firmly. "Even death."

And kissed her.